FICTION
Dek

Dekeyser, Stacy.

One witch at a time

DUE DATE	MCN	02/15	16.99

TWEEN FICTION DE

One
witch
at
a
time

One witch at a time

Stacy DeKeyser

Margaret K. McElderry Books

New York London Toronto Sydney New Delhi

MARGARET K. McELDERRY BOOKS

An imprint of Simon & Schuster Children's Publishing Division

1230 Avenue of the Americas, New York, New York 10020

MARGARET K. McELDERRY BOOKS is a trademark of Simon & Schuster, Inc.

For information about special discounts for bulk purchases, please contact Simon & Schuster Special Sales at 1-866-506-1949 or business@simonandschuster.com.

The Simon & Schuster Speakers Bureau can bring authors to your live event. For more information or to book an event, contact the Simon & Schuster Speakers Bureau at 1-866-248-3049 or visit our website at www.simonspeakers.com.

Book design by Sonia Chaghatzbanian

The text for this book is set in Bulmer.

Manufactured in the United States of America

0115 FFG

10 9 8 7 6 5 4 3 2 1

CIP data for this book is available from the Library of Congress.

ISBN 978-1-4814-1351-0 (hardcover)

ISBN 978-1-4814-1353-4 (eBook)

FIRST
EDITION

for Michaela

1

The boy hurried along the road as quickly as he could manage while tugging the hand of a squirmy girl.

"Slow down, Rudi!" the girl called.

But Rudi would not slow down. Why had he ever agreed to bring Susanna Louisa in the first place? Here he was, racing home to intercept a thief, who at this very moment might be raiding the farm. Taking his family's most prized possession. All because of a foolish bargain made by a nine-year-old girl.

"Please, Rudi! I'm hot! I'm thirsty! I'm tired!"

Rudi cursed under his breath. Then, over his shoulder: "You got us into this trouble, Susanna. Now you'll come with me to make it right." And he pulled her along without breaking pace.

•••

The day had started so well.

It had been a perfect spring morning, promising to be bright and warm. Dominating the ring of mountains that sheltered the village of Brixen, the black peak of the Berg reached into the cloudless sky like a knife poised to strike a crystal goblet.

Rudi Bauer had set out early, planning to arrive in Klausen before midmorning. It was the first market day of the year, and now that he was thirteen, Rudi would be venturing there on his own for the first time.

Before starting his journey, Rudi stopped at the fountain in the town square to fill his water skin. And, in a stroke of unlucky timing, there was Susanna Louisa. Before he knew it he had a companion, and they were trooping up the road together.

"I've never been to the spring market. I've never even been to Klausen. Thank you for letting me come, Rudi."

He glanced at her sidelong. Somehow he couldn't tell her, "Your mother paid me half a penny to take you," so instead he mumbled, "You're welcome." He gave one last halfhearted try. "Are you sure you want to come?"

"Oh, yes, Rudi. I want to see the market. Do you suppose there will be lambs? I'd love to see the lambs."

"The lambs in Klausen are no different from the lambs in Brixen."

"How do I know that, unless I see for myself? Besides, Mama says I should make myself useful. I'm going to sell these." She held out a huge basket. "Hildy laid them. She's my very own hen, so I'm allowed to sell her eggs."

After a moment's searching through a basketful of straw, Rudi finally found, at the very bottom, two brown eggs. They shimmered like gold in the dewy morning light.

He sighed. "If you want to be useful, why not stay home and help your mama with the new baby?"

Susanna Louisa hopped along, sending her basket swinging dangerously. "That won't do. Mama says I'm never so useful as when I'm outside in the fresh air. What are you taking to sell, Rudi?"

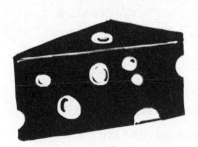

"Dairy stuff," he said, adjusting the pack on his back. "Cheeses. Butter." Even a dairyman's son could hardly make three meals a day of cheese and butter. Rudi was hoping to trade for cured meat, or grain, or both. He swallowed hard and cleared his throat. "I'm allowed to sell a cow, if I can strike a good bargain."

Susanna stopped and looked around. "What cow?"

Rudi bit back a sharp remark.

"The buyer will come back to the farm to get a cow. If I can strike a good bargain."

"But don't you need your cows, Rudi? Mama said you lost two cows already this winter, and now you have only three. Mama says three cows don't make a dairy."

"We're fine," Rudi said, perhaps a little too quickly. "Anyway, that's why I'm going to market today instead of Papa. Rosie will be calving any day now, and he needs to attend to her. So, you see? We're fine." Then, as if to betray his lie, Rudi's empty stomach rumbled so loudly he was sure it echoed off the Berg.

They finally arrived at the market on the outskirts of Klausen, and quickly became separated in the jostle of the crowd. Rudi guessed that Susanna would turn up at the nearest sheep pen, but he grumbled at himself. He'd been paid half a penny to watch her, after all, and already he'd lost sight of her.

He made his way through the busy marketplace, pushing past stalls displaying cabbages and rabbit skins and slabs of cured meat. Worry soon gave way to hunger, and so he traded a precious wedge of cheese for a slice of fried bacon and a roll of bread. Before long his stomach quieted, and he began to enjoy himself.

Rudi loved the Klausen market. For one rare day he was surrounded by people he didn't know. Most of them had traveled no more than a day's walk, and so they were practically his neighbors. But in this small corner of the world, even the next village seemed a foreign land. Rudi felt proud to be here on his own. He would make such a smart trade that Papa would send him every market day. And then he would be not simply Rudi Bauer, the dairyman's son. He would be Rudi Bauer, world traveler and shrewd trader.

But a world traveler probably ought not lose track of his companion, no matter how flighty she was. Rudi tucked away his last bit of bread and bacon for Susanna and continued his search for her.

"And don't come back, you scruffy waif!" called a voice. It belonged to a woman in the greengrocer's stall, who was shaking a bunch of spring onions. "I'll have no beggars or charlatans here!"

With an uneasy feeling, Rudi let his gaze follow the direction the onions were pointing. A girl hurried away between the stalls, but it was not Susanna Louisa. In fact, though he could not see her face, Rudi knew instantly that this girl was not from Brixen or any of the neighboring villages. Instead of the simple boiled wool that was the custom in the Brixen Valley, her long coat was made of stitched shearling and trimmed with fur. Despite the warm day, mittens dangled from strings at the ends of her sleeves. And instead of the braids that the local girls wore, her hair fell loose around her shoulders. Hair the color of a shiny copper florin.

Rudi followed the girl.

Now she approached the butcher's stall, holding out a hand and uttering words that Rudi could not hear. The butcher, a large man in a crisp white apron, shook a thick finger at her in reply. She drew her coat around herself and turned away.

Rudi's curiosity melted into a pang of sympathy. He felt out of place himself here in Klausen, among so many people he didn't know. And he was only an hour's walk from home. How lonely must this foreign girl feel, especially being met with such scorn?

Rudi stepped forward.

"P-pardon me . . . ," he stammered, feeling his face grow warm. "Is there something I can do? I mean, if you're hungry . . ." He reached into his pocket for the bread and bacon he'd been saving for Susanna.

"Hungry?" said the girl, as if surprised by Rudi's words, or perhaps it was his abrupt introduction. "You think I was begging, yes? Not begging. I can offer goods in trade." She glanced around her, as if looking for someone, and she shifted her weight from one foot to the other. "It doesn't look like much, but it's more than it seems."

Rudi guessed that she was about thirteen, like himself. How far had she traveled? Her boots were caked with mud, and so was the hem of her shearling coat. Her face was sunburned, and her bright hair was tangled into knots. Her brown eyes . . .

. . . were fixed on him, waiting for an answer. "If you

please? I am hungry, I'll confess. But I'm not begging, mind you. I have goods to trade."

He cleared his throat and tried to pretend his face was not burning. "I'm Rudolf Augustin Bauer, from the dairy in Brixen. I have the finest cheeses for sale or trade."

The girl curtsied with stiff politeness but did not introduce herself, as Rudi had hoped she would. "You are quite kind. I can pay you. It doesn't look like much, but it's more than it seems." The girl held out her hand, revealing precisely what she meant to pay.

Rudi's mouth fell open at the sight. He stared, and then he sputtered. "Sorry," he blurted. "There's been a . . . misunderstanding." He pushed the bread and bacon into the girl's hand and hurried off.

No wonder the greengrocer and butcher had been insulted. Rudi might be the son of a dairy farmer from a tiny village in the mountains, but he was no rube. So she was hungry. He was hungry too, but fair was fair. He could not afford to trade his wares for nothing, not even to a lost-looking foreign girl with exquisite red hair and liquid brown eyes. Rudi stalked through the marketplace, muttering to himself.

After a few minutes' wandering and muttering, Rudi came upon a sheep pen, and there was Susanna Louisa.

"Rudi!" she cried, bouncing up to him. "I have something to tell you!"

He noticed that her basket was empty. "You sold your eggs?"

"No, I dropped them. But something else! I sold your cow for you, and now you'll never be hungry again!" She held out her hand, and Rudi saw that she was holding exactly what the foreign girl had offered him only a few minutes before.

Rudi felt the blood drain from his face. "You sold one of our cows for *that*?"

She nodded, looking very pleased. "I told her she could come to your farm this very day. Isn't that wonderful?"

"No! It's not! Our cows are not yours to sell! How could you be so stupid? How could you trade an entire cow for *that*?" Rudi jabbed a finger at her open hand. "For a . . . a handful of *beans*?"

Susanna's smile faded. She regarded the pile of dried beans in her hand. Then she lifted her chin in indignation. "Rudi. I am not stupid. I would not trade a beautiful cow for a bunch of plain old beans. But these are not plain old beans. These . . ." She held them up to his nose. "These are *magic* beans."

2

"Come with me." Rudi pulled Susanna Louisa through the marketplace, frantic to find the foreign girl and undo what Susanna had done.

"Don't you want your beans?" Susanna Louisa called out.

"No!"

The red-haired girl was nowhere to be found, but she had left a trail of gossip in her wake.

"She tried to trade a pocketful of pole beans for one of my best cabbages," said the greengrocer's wife with a scowl. "I can't do business like that. I sent her on her way."

The butcher told a similar tale. "I has no use for such lunking great beans. Even a soup bone requires a fair trade." He shook his head. "She wore shearling, did you see that? Didn't think such folk ventured this side of the mountains."

At every stall Rudi and Susanna heard the same story: a furtive, foreign girl had approached, hoping to trade a handful of dried beans for a loaf of bread, or a smoked sausage, or a sack of apples. But no one had been gullible enough to make such a trade (except, of course, Susanna Louisa), and now it seemed the stranger herself was gone.

There was nothing to do but race home and hope to arrive before the girl did. Or, if they were lucky, they'd catch up with her on the road.

But they would not be lucky. Susanna Louisa could barely keep pace. And Rudi's pack was still heavy. He'd never had the chance to sell his goods at the market, and now they were only weighing him down.

"I can't, Rudi!" cried Susanna. She pulled out of his grasp and collapsed, breathless, by the side of the road.

He handed over his skin of water, and she drank in huge gulps. "Please, Susanna. I know it's far, but we must get home. If that girl takes a cow, we'll be ruined for sure!"

Just then Rudi heard a clattering along the road, coming toward them from the direction of the market-place.

A wagon. And instead of a lumbering slow draft horse, it was being pulled by a sprightly pony at a brisk pace. In desperate hope, Rudi stepped into the road and waved his arms.

The driver reined his pony to a halt and regarded Rudi with a squint. "Here now, what's all this? I could've run you over."

Rudi hurried around the pony. "Are you going toward Brixen? We need to get to Brixen!"

"Brixen? I has no business there. I'm on my way to the abbey of Saint Adolphus. I'm to load casks of ale to sell at market for the Adolphine brothers."

Rudi's heart sank. The abbey was nowhere near Brixen. But he would never get home quickly enough on foot. He searched his brain for a solution, and found one—he hoped.

He wiggled his knapsack off his shoulders. "I can pay you. A pack full of cheese and butter if you'll give us a ride to Brixen." It was a desperately high price to pay, but this was a desperate situation.

The driver rubbed his chin and chewed his cheek. He craned his neck and regarded the sun, as if to gauge the time.

Rudi tried again. "Please? I'm sure the good brothers would enjoy a supply of fresh butter and cheese." He held his breath, waiting for an answer.

Finally the driver cocked his head toward the wagon. "Hurry up, then."

With a yelp of relief, Rudi hoisted his pack onto the

wagon, and then helped Susanna Louisa. He climbed up next, and they were off.

After a few moments' silence, Susanna Louisa spoke. "Don't worry, Rudi. We haven't seen the foreign girl on the road, so maybe she went the other direction. I never did tell her where you live."

Rudi's stomach dropped as he realized his own error. "No. But I did."

And there it was. He could blame Susanna Louisa for being foolish, but it did nothing to change the truth: The fault was all his own. He was the one who had begged Papa to let him go to the market in Klausen. He was the one who had assured Mama that he could strike a fair bargain, and now he had traded a month's worth of butter and cheese for a ride on a wagon. He was the one who'd lost sight of Susanna Louisa when he'd promised he would mind her.

How had things gotten so bad so quickly?

Rudi reminded himself that nothing could be worse than last summer. When all the children of Brixen—all except Rudi—had been lured away by the enchanted music of an evil fiddler. Rudi had found his friends and brought them safely home, but only with the help of the old woman on the mountain.

Of course, she was more than just an old woman. She was Brixen's very own witch. But it was bad luck to talk of such things. And yet, perhaps too many villagers had done just that, for the winter had been especially harsh, even for the mountains. All of Brixen had suffered, but none worse than those at the Bauer farm. Papa's supply of winter feed had become buried in the drifting snow, and then it had rotted. One by one the cows had starved. Rudi had worried that before the winter was out, he and his family might starve too.

Now it was spring and the snows had melted, except for the shadiest patches. Rudi had insisted on carrying everything he could to the first market day in Klausen, in an effort to replenish the larder at home.

Instead he was returning empty-handed, and who knew what he would find at home? One less cow, a furious Papa, a distraught Mama. And Oma, who would be shaking her head at his foolishness.

"It'll be all right, Rudi," said Susanna Louisa, who must have seen the despair on his face. "I'm sure your papa will know what to do. He'll give that girl the worst cow. The bad-tempered one who always kicks the milk bucket."

Rudi groaned under his breath. And though he knew it would do no good, he couldn't help saying what was on his mind. "You were tricked, Susanna. That girl told you a wild story about magic beans so she could get a cow for nothing." His heart sank at the thought. He had felt sorry for the shearling girl. He had almost begun to like her.

"I was not tricked!" Susanna protested. "These beans are worth a hundred cows, if you ask me. They'll grow wherever you plant them. And they'll sprout so many beans that everyone in Brixen will have their fill."

"I suppose the foreign girl told you that, too?"

"She didn't need to," said Susanna. "What else would magic beans do?"

Her words hung in the air for a long moment. Then, with a creeping realization, Rudi turned toward Susanna Louisa. "So, the girl didn't *say* they were magic beans?"

Susanna patted him patiently on the arm. "Rudi. It's not something you say *out loud*. Think of the great huge fuss it would cause."

An unexpected glimmer of relief kept Rudi's frustration from boiling over. He squinted at Susanna as they bumped along the road. "What about the cow, then? Did she ask you for a cow?"

"Oh no," said Susanna with pride. "That was my idea."

"Your idea? *Why?*"

"Because, Rudi! You can't trade magic beans for just anything!" She sounded as exasperated as Rudi felt.

And so the truth was out. Rudi forced himself to take one deep breath, and then he spoke as evenly as he could. "You took it upon yourself to give away one of our last three cows for . . . for nothing."

She blinked up at him in hurt indignation. "It's not nothing!"

The pony and cart rounded the last bend in the road. Ahead lay the River Brix with its footbridge; and beyond it, the Bauer farm on the edge of Brixen. Rudi strained to watch and listen for activity at the farm: any bustling or shouting or lowing of cows. But all was quiet. Rudi wasn't sure if he should be relieved or worried.

The cart came to a stop at the footbridge. "You'll have to walk from here," said the driver. "Good luck with them beans of yours." He winked at Rudi and left them standing at the side of the road.

"See that?" said Rudi. "I'm not the only one who thinks you were gullible."

Susanna Louisa narrowed her eyes at him. "What's gullible? Stupid? I told you already, I'm not stupid." Her mouth became a thin line, and her eyes filled with tears.

Rudi gulped, and despite all the trouble she had caused, his heart softened. "No, not stupid. Just . . . too trusting." He swallowed his pride and offered his hand.

But Susanna Louisa sidestepped Rudi and stomped away across the bridge. Then she turned, swiped at her eyes, and reached into the pocket of her pinafore. Without a word, she drew out one bean and held it up for Rudi to see. Then she flung the bean toward the riverbank, where it bounced once and became lost in the soft new grass. She plopped onto the ground, planted her chin on her fists, and stared at the spot.

Rudi blinked at her. If an angry look were enough to make a bean sprout, Susanna Louisa was the one to make it happen. He shook his head and left her to watch over her bean. She knew her way home from here. He needed to see what kind of damage had been done at the farm.

3

Just as Rudi had imagined, his grandmother stood waiting in the doorway of the cottage, tapping her foot.

"How did you fare at market?" she said. "You traded for something tasty, I hope."

Rudi hurried through the gate. "Has anyone been here, Oma? A red-haired foreign girl with muddy boots?"

Oma raised an eyebrow. "You traded for a foreign girl? I was hoping for something more like a ham."

"Oma!" Rudi tugged at his collar, which suddenly felt tight. "Have you seen such a girl? Wearing a heavy thick shearling coat?"

Now both her eyebrows lifted. "Shearling? No. I've seen no one all day."

Mama stepped outside. "Home so soon, Rudi? But

your knapsack looks empty. Did you bring nothing home in exchange for all that cheese and butter?"

"He traded it for a shearling girl," said Oma. "I hope she knows how to milk a cow."

"The cows!" cried Rudi, forgetting everything else. "Has anyone come to claim a cow?"

"Did you sell a cow after all?" said Mama. She shook her head, as if to clear her thoughts. "Perhaps I heard you wrong. Perhaps you said that someone will deliver *us* a cow. In trade for the goods you carried to market?"

"I never made a trade with anyone!" said Rudi. And then, eager to explain how the day's events were not all his fault, he told them everything. How Susanna Louisa had taken it upon herself to offer one of their precious cows for a handful of dried beans.

"I must tell Papa," said Mama, her hands fluttering. "Rosie calved this morning. A fine little heifer, and we'll not trade her for such a pittance." She hurried off in the direction of the barn.

Oma shook her head. "Foolish child," she muttered.

"She meant well . . . ," Rudi said. After all, Susanna Louisa was only nine years old.

"I'm talking about you!" snapped Oma. "I want to see these beans."

Grateful for a chance to escape, Rudi dashed away to find Susanna Louisa.

She was still sitting on the riverbank, chin in her hands, staring at the spot where she had thrown the bean.

Though he wanted to, Rudi did not scoff at Susanna. He did not tell her how silly she was to sit and wait for a seed to grow. He only tugged at her arm. "My Oma wants a word with you." Then, to soften the blow of the scolding that awaited her, he added, "Do you want to mark the spot with a stick or something?"

Susanna shot him a look. "I don't need to." She stood, brushed bits of grass from her pinafore, and flounced up the lane and toward the Bauer cottage.

Oma was waiting inside, rocking in her chair.

"Good day, mistress," said Susanna Louisa with a quick curtsy.

Oma gave a nod and held out her hand. "Let's see these beans of yours."

Susanna dug into the pocket of her pinafore. "They're not mine, mistress. They're yours. I'm only holding them in safekeeping." She gave Rudi a sidelong glare as she handed them over.

Oma squinted at the pile of dried beans in her hand. "Hmm." She pushed the beans toward Rudi. "What do you see?"

Rudi studied the hard white beans with their black

marks. He shrugged. "They're ordinary soldier beans. Most years we have whole sacks of them."

Oma shook her head. "These are bigger than soldier beans. And the markings are different." She took one bean and held it up for Rudi. "What do you see?"

"A keyhole shape," offered Susanna helpfully.

She was right. The mark on the bean looked like a perfectly formed keyhole. Rudi took another bean from Oma's hand, and another. And another. Without variation, they all had the same mark.

He scratched behind his ear. "Maybe they're a new strain. Keyhole beans?"

Together, Oma and Susanna said, *"Hmph."*

Rudi blinked at them, and then a realization dawned. "You can't be saying they really are magic?"

Oma snatched the beans from Rudi's hand and slipped them into her apron pocket. "I will do the safekeeping now, if you don't mind." Then to Susanna she said, "Hurry on home now, child. You've been very useful, thank you."

Susanna nodded. "My mother likes me to be useful." She gave Rudi one last satisfied look and skipped out the door.

Oma waited until they were alone, and then she shook a finger at Rudi.

"Have you forgotten everything you've learned?

Spouting off about magic. You know it's bad luck to talk of such things!"

"But, Oma!" And then he lowered his voice, though no one else was in the house. "Those beans can't be magic!"

"Why not?"

"B-because . . . ," he sputtered. "Because as a rule, things are *not* magic." It was like trying to explain why Rosie had birthed a calf and not a lamb. Of all people, Oma should understand such things.

But she only said, "It's easier to prove what *is* than to prove what is *not*."

Rudi swallowed his exasperation. "If the beans were magic, something would have happened at the riverbank."

"At the riverbank? What sort of something?"

Rudi explained how Susanna Louisa had tossed one of the beans, expecting for all the world that it would sprout before her eyes. But it had not sprouted then, and Rudi was certain it had not sprouted since.

Oma fixed a steady eye on him. "You think these beans are nothing but a poor excuse for supper. But *I* think they're trouble." She rocked for a moment, thinking. "There's one way to know for sure. Someone needs to take them to the witch."

With a gulp, Rudi peered out at the stark black peak of the Berg, which loomed above Brixen like a storm cloud. He knew that by "someone," Oma meant *him*.

He was not afraid to climb the mountain. He was not afraid of the Brixen Witch. Ever since that day last summer, when he and the witch had worked together to foil the evil fiddler and rescue the children of Brixen, Rudi had hoped to see her again.

But he had hoped it would be a sociable visit. He would take off his boots and share stories, and tea, and elderberry tarts. He had not planned on making another pitiable plea for help. What would she think of him, getting into trouble again so soon?

He sighed. "When shall I go? Now?"

Oma squinted at the sun, which rested on the peak of the Berg in the western sky. Soon the valley would be enveloped in the mountain's cold shadow.

"In the morning," she declared. "At first light. And you'll take the tanner's child with you."

Rudi groaned. "Susanna? She'll only slow me down or get lost."

"You're going to need her." Oma scooped the beans from her pocket and examined them again in the light of the fire. "Susanna Louisa may be a pest, but she's a pest who knows a magic bean when she sees one."

4

Rudi grumbled to himself as he lay in bed that night, thinking about the errand he did not want to run. He grumbled as he rose the next morning, when the light outside the window softened from black to the palest gray. He grumbled as he pulled on his boots and wrapped the last of Mama's elderberry tarts.

"Are you sure this is a good idea?" he whispered to Oma once Mama was out of earshot. "That foreign girl must surely be coming for the cow today."

"Your papa can deal with things here," said Oma, handing him a small pouch. "You have a job to do."

"I still say these beans are not magic." Nonetheless, he pocketed the pouch.

"You'll find out soon enough," said Oma. "If, on your way up the mountain, you see that the bean has sprouted on the riverbank overnight, you can tell the witch that there's magic hereabout."

Rudi collected his knapsack. "And if it hasn't sprouted?"

"Then you can tell her that perhaps the magic is biding its time."

"But, Oma—"

Just then the door swung open and Papa stepped in, wiping his feet. His clothes were rumpled, and a bit of straw was stuck in his hair.

"Good morning, Son," said Oma. "And how is our newborn doing?"

"Mother and calf are doing well," said Papa, sitting and pulling off his boots. "The new spring grass will help Rosie's milk come in nicely. Mayhaps the harsh months are finally behind us, and it's about time."

"Look at you, poor dear!" said Mama, coming down the stairs. "Spent the whole night in the barn. Did you get a moment's rest for yourself?"

Papa rubbed his head, sending bits of straw floating to the floor. "Slept like a baby, truth be told. Ordinarily I can't get a wink in the barn at night, what with the cows lowing and Zick-Zack prowling for mice. But it was quiet as a church all night. More peaceful than in my own bed, I'd venture to say. Not that you snore so loudly, Mama." He winked at Rudi.

"See where you sleep tonight," was Mama's reply, and then, "Such an odd thing about Zick-Zack. I hope she hasn't been snatched by a hawk or a wolf." And then Mama gasped. "Or gone off to be a witch's cat," she whispered.

Oma snorted. "Cats favoring witches? It's a silly superstition. As for the hawks and wolves, they're the ones need to worry about Zick-Zack, not the other way 'round." She cast a troubled glance at Rudi, though she didn't say another word.

Papa shrugged out of his coat. "She'll turn up. I'll wager she was out hunting on the meadow or some such. Rudi! Where are you off to so early?" He spied the package in Rudi's hand. "Ah, elderberry tarts. So it's up the mountain for you, to beg for help undoing your reckless bargain? Off with you, then. Tell the . . . old woman . . . that we can't be expected to trade one of our precious lovely cows for a meager handful of beans."

Despite Papa's stinging words, Rudi couldn't help noticing an interesting conundrum: Papa was content to have Rudi seek the counsel of the old woman on the mountain, even while he would not admit that the old woman and the Brixen Witch were one and the same. *It's bad luck to talk of such things.* Because to talk of such things meant admitting such things. It meant admitting that the village of Brixen was not only at the mercy of the weather and the seasons and the occasional pushy monarch. It was at the mercy of its very own witch.

Rudi was grateful for the witch, and he knew Papa was too. Brixen was at her mercy, it was true. But she was also their protector. That was one more thing Rudi had learned not so long ago.

"No foreigner will take any cow of ours," said Oma, tucking the bundle of tarts into Rudi's knapsack. "'Twould be folly, trying to lead a creature through the mountains this time of year. It's time someone visited the poor woman, that's all. See how she fared the winter."

And now Rudi realized the true reason Oma was sending him up the mountain. She didn't think the beans were magic any more than he did. It was only an excuse to check on the witch, who was very old and perhaps a bit frail, and who had endured a harsh winter the same as they had. Rudi decided that he would go gladly. It would be a boots-off, tea-and-tart sort of visit after all.

He retrieved his coat from behind the door. "I'm off, then. I'll see you tonight."

"Be careful." Mama lifted his cap and smoothed his hair, which was her way of saying good-bye, now that he was thirteen and too old to be kissed by his mother.

"Good luck, Son," said Papa, placing a hand on Rudi's shoulder. "And keep an eye out for wolf-eating cats."

Rudi made his way through the village and toward

the tanner's cottage. The steeple clock struck the early hour, and in the distance the blacksmith's hammer rang. Rudi sniffed the air for a hint of baking bread, but he smelled only the sharpness of wood smoke.

Now he felt a pang of guilt. If Susanna Louisa had been tempted into accepting beans that she thought would feed the entire village, could he blame her? She was nine years old. She had only been trying to help.

Hungry or not, the villagers of Brixen were a hardy lot, and so they went about their day as usual. Or so it seemed to the casual eye, but Rudi knew better. Small children stared as he drew near, and were nudged behind their mothers' skirts. The matrons smiled awkwardly, and the menfolk gave stiff nods. Rudi tried to ignore the sidelong glances. He told himself he did not hear whispering behind his back.

At the edge of the village square, Rudi came upon Mistress Gerta scrubbing her doorstep. She was a widow with many children—so many, in fact, that she could scarcely keep their names straight. As for children who were not her own, Mistress Gerta never bothered with names. Any girl was called "Sweet," and any boy was called "Lad."

And so Rudi blinked in surprise when she said to him, as clear as day, "Good morning, Master Rudi."

He gave a wary nod as he walked past. "Good day, mistress."

"Rudi!" His friend Konrad raced across the square, with his little brother Roger close behind.

"Hullo, Rudi!" Roger's wide grin revealed two missing teeth. "Mama says we're not supposed to talk to you."

"Why not?" demanded Rudi, though he knew perfectly well why not, and it vexed him. "Besides, you *are* talking to me."

"Mama also says we should be nice to you," explained Roger. "Because you're friends with the wi—"

Konrad clapped a hand over his brother's mouth, but Roger kicked him in the shin. "How can we be nice to Rudi if we don't talk to him?" said Roger, scowling.

Konrad rubbed his sore leg. "Where are you going, Rudi?"

Rudi scratched his ear. "To the tanner's cottage. To pick up a package." Which was true, more or less.

"We'll come with you," said Konrad, to Rudi's exasperation. On any other day he would have welcomed the company. But not today.

"Mama says we have chores!" declared Roger, and Rudi took the chance to bid a hasty farewell.

At the far end of the village was the blacksmith's shop. Its forge glowed with heat, and Marco the smith swung his hammer, striking the anvil in a series of CLANGs that pierced the air. Without breaking his rhythm, Marco gave Rudi a grin and a knowing wink.

Rudi sighed. At least Marco wasn't uneasy around him.

Now the clanging stopped, and Marco stepped away from his forge. "Ah, my favorite thief!"

Rudi's face grew hot, and it wasn't from the heat of the forge. "Master Smith," he muttered, "I never stole . . . anything." He'd almost said, "I never stole the witch's gold coin," but he'd held his tongue just in time. "At least not on purpose. You know that."

Marco clapped Rudi on the back. "Don't be so modest!" He leaned closer. "Nothing wrong with embellishing the truth a bit, lad. It builds a healthy respect. I've been thinking of taking on an apprentice. Interested?"

"Me?" said Rudi. "Oh, I couldn't. My papa needs me. And I like the dairy. But thank you for asking, all the same."

"Where are you off to?"

After a moment's hesitation Rudi invented an errand, and surprised himself at his own words. "I'm off to unlock something. I think." It must have been the thought of the keyhole beans tucked deep inside his pocket.

Marco lifted an eyebrow. "You don't say. Have you got the right key?"

Rudi shrugged. "I don't think it's that sort of lock."

"Wouldn't be much of a lock if it didn't need a

key," said the blacksmith. "Wait here." He disappeared into his shed. A moment later he was back, and he pressed something heavy and cold into Rudi's palm. "A skeleton key. It will open all but the most devious lock." Marco gave him a nudge. "Or you could always throw it. It's solid enough to raise a welt, I've no doubt."

Rudi regarded the iron key, which was nearly as long as his hand. He couldn't imagine needing it for either purpose. Still, he nodded his thanks and slipped the key into his pocket.

Now Rudi came upon the tanner's cottage. He hesitated, wishing he could go up the mountain by himself. But Oma was not someone he could easily disobey. He steeled himself and banged on the door.

A moment later, Mistress Tanner stood in the doorway with a squalling bundle in her arms. "Good morning, Master Rudi," she said, not quite looking him in the eye.

This was the way of things now: a wink and a nod. A wary sort of courtesy. Being called "Master Rudi" or "my favorite thief!" All because he had met the witch. He had almost gotten used to such treatment, but he still didn't like it.

Just now it made him feel itchy all over, which

meant he must be blushing. "Good day, mistress," he said, with an awkward touch of his cap. "My grandmother has sent me with a message."

After several minutes of discussing, cajoling, and solemn assurances passed along from Oma, the matter was decided, and Susanna Louisa appeared on the doorstep wearing her traveling coat.

"No one but your grandmother could talk me into such a thing, after what happened up there last summer." Mistress Tanner shuddered. "But if she says it must be done, then I suppose it must. Off you go, then, before I change my mind." She pulled her daughter close and kissed her upon the head. Then, holding the squalling bundle tightly to her chest, she disappeared inside the cottage.

Susanna Louisa grabbed Rudi's hand, though he had not offered it. "Isn't this exciting? Going up the mountain to visit that nice old woman again."

"So you remember her?" observed Rudi.

"Oh, yes. That day last summer when that nasty mean fiddler sealed us up inside the mountain. She chased him away forever. After *you* rescued us." Susanna squeezed Rudi's hand in gratitude. "I wonder why she lives up there, so near the witch?"

Rudi tugged his hand out of Susanna's. "You know, Susanna," he said carefully, "there are not *two* old women living up on the Berg."

Susanna frowned in thought. Finally her eyes widened, and the words spilled out in a hoarse whisper. "You mean to say the old woman *is* the Brixen Witch?"

He nodded and put a finger to his lips.

"No wonder Mama was worried." Susanna grabbed Rudi's hand once more, and pulled him along the lane. "Let's go!"

5

"**Susanna,**" **said Rudi** as they made their way through the village, "aren't you afraid of the witch?"

"Oh, no," Susanna replied. "I know she's fearsome when she sends storms and such, but she's only doing her job. Like when Mama says, 'Are you jumble-headed, Susanna Louisa? I told you to bring that washing in off the line yesterday!'" She stopped midstep. "Oops."

Rudi stopped too. "What?"

"I was supposed to bring the washing in off the line yesterday. Oh well!" She tossed a braid over her shoulder and set off again down the lane. "To think I've already met the witch and didn't even know it! And now I'll have another chance. Isn't that nice, Rudi?"

Now it was Rudi's turn to stop short.

Few people ever made the acquaintance of the Brixen Witch. Oma had, sometime long before Rudi had been born. He himself had stumbled upon the witch's doorstep, quite literally, when he had found her enchanted coin last year. But very few people wanted such familiarity.

Now he regarded Susanna Louisa. "You *want* to meet the witch again? Why?"

"Why not?"

Rudi sighed. He tried again, choosing his words carefully. "It's a tricky thing, getting to know the witch. It brings . . . responsibility." He thought about the wash line. And then he remembered Mistress Tanner's "Good morning, Master Rudi" and the itchy feeling it had caused. "People will think of you differently. They may even become a tiny bit afraid of you."

"Oh, I'm not worried," said Susanna. "After all, I'm not afraid of *you*. Will we see the Witch's Chair today, Rudi? I'd really like to see the Witch's Chair."

Rudi squinted up at the mountain. "I suppose so. If the weather is favorable."

High on the Berg stood a rocky outcropping. It had

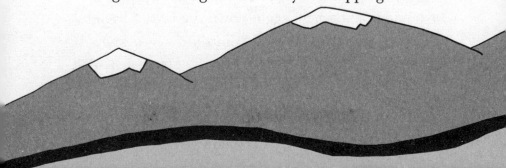

been formed eons ago by the forces of the earth, and it looked just like a chair. For that reason—and because it was deep in the Brixen Witch's realm—it was called the Witch's Chair. Legend said that those who sat upon it would be met with the witch herself. Some considered this a blessing; most considered it a curse. More than ever, Rudi considered it might be both.

They passed through the village gates. Just beyond lay the near meadow, and the River Brix and its footbridge. "My bean!" exclaimed Susanna, and she hurried toward the bridge. With a queasy curiosity, Rudi quickened his pace and followed her.

Susanna Louisa stood on the footbridge, staring at the riverbank. Rudi stepped up behind her, and his gaze followed hers.

On the riverbank Rudi saw waves of soft spring grass, and the first yellow dots of dandelions, and tender rushes poking up at the edge of the water.

Susanna Louisa sighed. "No bean plant." She looked up at Rudi. "Now what?"

Rudi shrugged and pulled her away from the bridge. "Now we tell the witch that perhaps the magic is biding its time."

And so they walked—the lanky, serious boy and the knobby-kneed, chatty girl—across the near meadow, where Papa's meager dairy herd was munching hungrily at the new grass. Through the chilly shade of the forest, where the blanket of pine needles muffled every step. Up toward the high meadow, following the switchback trail across the steep slope. Past the treacherous field of scree, where Rudi had lost a magic gold coin many months before.

Rudi thought about the beans he carried in his pocket. He still doubted they held any magic, but their keyhole markings proved they were no ordinary beans. Susanna Louisa had been the one to notice that.

And in her turn, Oma had noticed something in Susanna Louisa. An inclination? A talent? Rudi didn't quite know the right word. Whatever it was, Oma clearly thought it was something the Brixen Witch should know about.

Rudi watched Susanna now. She jostled along beside him with her coat unbuttoned, kicking at patches of lingering snow, examining puddles for pollywogs, showing not the least hint of fatigue or worry. If she had a talent for conferring with such folk as witches, she did not show it. And if this place stirred up within her the same dreadful memories it did for Rudi, she did not show that, either.

"Remember last summer, Rudi? When that nasty mean fiddler came? I can't recall a thing about following him up the mountain, but we must have, because we hiked down this way afterward. Remember, Rudi?"

Rudi gulped and rubbed his hands on his trousers. "Yes, Susanna. I remember."

They were on the high meadow now. Dwindling fields of snow clung to the shady spots—the last remnants of the long and brutal winter. The air was fragrant with the first wildflowers of the Alpine spring. Rudi and Susanna turned up their collars to the biting wind, which was always present here, high on the mountain. But the sun was strong, and it warmed their faces even as the wind bit their cheeks.

Susanna Louisa gasped. "There it is!" she cried, and she broke into a run.

The Witch's Chair.

Rudi decided it was no use trying to stop her. Perhaps she was meant to climb up and sit there, after all. Who was he to get in the way of that?

"Give me a boost," she said, and in a moment she was up. She settled herself on the slab of rock, stretching her legs. "Are you coming up, Rudi?"

Rudi shook his head. This was not a playground, after all. It was a place that required respect.

Now Susanna Louisa pointed excitedly. "There's Brixen! The whole village! It's so tiny and far away!"

She waved a greeting that no one would see.

"We should keep going," said Rudi. "It's not far now."

Susanna Louisa scrambled off the rock and brushed at her skirt, which was already too muddy to be brushed clean. "What will the witch do about the beans, Rudi? Do you think she knows who the foreign girl is? My mama says that while we're there, we should ask her to take pity on Brixen after such a nasty winter. And you should ask her for more cows. What else shall we ask the witch for, Rudi?"

He shook his head. "I don't think it works that way."

"My mama says it does. Everyone says it does."

Rudi wanted to say, "Everyone is superstitious and silly," but he held his tongue. He thought for a bit. "I think the witch is . . . more like a night watchman."

Susanna tugged at a braid. "You mean she sleeps all day, and snores so loudly that the windows rattle?"

Rudi stifled a laugh. "No. I just think that the witch knows things we don't. The same way the night watchman can see so well in the dark, and can hear faint noises. The way he stays alert while everyone else is sleeping. The night watchman doesn't *cause* a smoldering ember in a haystack to grow into a blazing fire. He's just the first to see it, and he warns everyone else. I think the witch is sort of like that."

Susanna Louisa skipped ahead of him on the path. "But that's not magic," she called back to him. "Doesn't the witch do any real magic?"

The path was steeper now, and Rudi stepped more carefully. "Oh, yes. There is real magic about the witch, no doubt. I'm only saying that—perhaps—some of what the witch does only *seems* like magic, because we don't pay attention as well as she does."

"I suppose that makes sense," said Susanna, stooping to pluck a handful of tiny pink rock jasmine. "How old is the witch, Rudi? Can I ask her about that, anyway?"

"I don't think you're supposed to ask such things," said Rudi, following her along the rocky path. He stopped for a moment to catch his breath. "I think we're almost there. Better hold on so you don't slip." And he reached out to take her hand.

But she was gone.

6

"Susanna?" Rudi turned in every direction, but she had vanished.

She could not have gone far. The high meadow was behind them, and now the path wound steeply toward the peak of the Berg. On one side, the sheer face of the mountain rose toward the sky. On the other side were scattered boulders, and just beyond them was—nothing. The mountain simply fell away on that side. Anyone who wandered more than a few steps off the path might never be seen again.

But Susanna Louisa was as sure-footed as a mountain goat, Rudi told himself. She had not slipped once on their journey so far.

"Susanna?" He steeled himself and peeked over the edge.

Nothing.

"Susanna Louisa? This isn't funny!"

She must have gone ahead on the trail. Of course. Rudi followed the path upslope once more and called her name, and swallowed a growing sense of panic.

There were stories of menacing things here, high on the Berg. Wolves. Lynxes. Unsavory travelers from the far side of the mountain. But those were only stories— or in any case, not likely. That's what Rudi told himself as he stepped warily along the trail. He reached into his pocket and felt the reassuring heft of Marco's key. He might need to throw it, after all.

Rudi crept around a bend. Ahead of him the path led directly through a tall, narrow crevice that split the black rock of the mountain in two.

He knew this place. Within that crevice lay the Brixen Witch's front door.

Rudi hurried forward into the cold shadow of the cleft. He stopped for a moment, blinking in the dim light. The bright sunshine at the far end of the crevice made the shadows all the darker. "Susanna? Are you here?"

Had she already found the witch's door and gone inside? Rudi crouched in the shade of the crevice, searching for the low door that led into the mountain. To the untrained eye, the door looked like only another facet of the rock, but Rudi knew better. He found the spot and he knocked.

But his knuckles made no sound. So he kicked at the rock. Once, twice—

And on the third kick Rudi's boot met nothing but air. His foot swept into a pocket of darkness—an open doorway that had not been there a moment before—and he landed on the ground with a thud.

Something stepped in from the bright sunshine of the path beyond the crevice and stood over him. It was Susanna Louisa, her braids swinging. "There you are!" she said.

Rudi scrambled to his feet. "I thought you fell off the mountain!" he growled, allowing his fear and relief to melt into anger.

"Why would I do that?" She gasped. "Look! You found something! Is it the witch's door? You go first." She pushed him through the open doorway.

The door slammed shut behind them, and they stood in utter darkness. Rudi straightened himself and tried to blink away the blackness. Something nudged him from behind; a small hand found his and grasped it tightly. He did not resist.

Now the small hand tugged at Rudi's. Instinctively he lowered his head.

"This was a good idea, right, Rudi?" came Susanna Louisa's wavering whisper.

"Oma said it was," he whispered back. "I suppose she must be right."

Now came a noise from deep within the cave. Footsteps. The small hand squeezed his so tightly, Rudi had to bite back a yelp.

He decided to set a brave example and announce himself. It was the polite thing to do, after all. Besides, he and the witch were old acquaintances. He opened his mouth to call "Hello!" but something happened to the word on its journey from his lungs to his lips, and the sound that emerged was more like a squeaky "'Lo?'"

The footsteps ceased. Something told Rudi that even though his own eyes could not yet see in the dark, other eyes could see him quite well.

"Wipe yer boots," said a voice, surprisingly close. Rudi automatically obeyed, and he could tell by the tugging on his hand that Susanna Louisa was doing the same.

Somewhere in the gloom a light flared brightly, and then it settled and softened. Rudi heard the creak of an iron grate, and gradually he saw the outline of a piped stove. Next to it stood the familiar shape of a small person in ragged skirts. He blinked, and as his eyes adjusted, her form took further shape.

Her shoulders were wrapped in a threadbare shawl. Tufts of white hair escaped from under a faded kerchief. Her face was crossed with a thousand lines, and her mouth was twisted into what might have been a grin. Or it might have been a grimace.

"So," she said without further introduction. "I were not expecting visitors again so soon. What has you brought me? Gifts? Offerings? Supplication?" The tiny old woman held out her hand.

Rudi was ready for this. He shrugged off his pack, pulled it open, and drew out a small package. "Elderberry tarts. Sorry there aren't many. It's been a . . . lean year."

"So it has," said the witch, unwrapping the package with care. "And how is your family, young Rudolf? Is Gussie well?" She broke off a bit of tart, nibbled it, and sighed contentedly.

"Oma is well, thank you, mistress," said Rudi. "Though we are all a bit thinner than last time I saw you." He hoped she couldn't hear his stomach. The sight of the tarts had sent it gurgling.

But if she noticed, she made no sign. Instead, she turned her attention to Susanna Louisa.

The two stood eyeing each other—the little girl and the littler witch. Despite her extra inch of height, Susanna Louisa took a halting step backward.

Rudi knew how she felt. He got the same squirmy feeling whenever the witch turned her full attention on him. It was something like stepping barefoot into a fresh cowpat—not entirely unpleasant while it was still warm, but someplace he'd rather not stay for more than a few seconds.

"Well, missy?" said the witch. "What about yourself?"

Susanna blinked. Then, remembering herself, she hitched a curtsy. "What *about* me, mistress?"

The witch held out her hand and tapped her foot. "Gifts? Supplication? It's how things is done hereabout."

Susanna Louisa cast a pitiful glance at Rudi. But before he could reply, her face brightened. She reached into her pinafore pocket, drew out the bunch of rock jasmine, and placed the jumble of tiny pink blossoms onto the witch's outstretched palm.

The witch regarded them with a raised eyebrow. "It'll do. Come in. Sit down."

Having been here before, Rudi knew the way of things. He stepped toward the glowing stove and perched himself on the low footstool that faced the solitary chair. Without prompting or complaint Susanna Louisa settled herself on the braided rug, tucking her gangly legs under her.

The witch stirred the fire, and now it warmed the air and chased the dampness. "I'm sorry I hasn't any tea to offer. It's been a lean year up here, too. Those blossoms you brought are lovely to smell, but I'm afraid they doesn't make a good tea."

"That's all right," said Rudi quickly. "We haven't come for tea." Which was true, strictly speaking. Still, he had held out a small hope for a steamy mug of her chamomile. He told himself it was just as well. A sip of tea would only make him crave a bite of tart, and he had brought too few to expect her to share.

The witch settled into her chair. "What has you come for, then? Are you in trouble again already?"

"Not *trouble*, exactly," Rudi said. "It's only—"

"It's these." Susanna Louisa nudged Rudi. He pulled the small pouch from his pocket and handed it to the witch.

"So," said the witch, her face crinkling into a grin, "you has one more little giftie for me?" She opened the pouch and peered inside.

"Oma said you might know what to do about them," said Rudi.

The witch emptied the contents of the pouch into one hand. "Do about them?" She frowned. "I has no place to plant a garden up here. And this is not even enough beans to make a proper soup."

Rudi leaned forward on the footstool and cleared his throat. "No, mistress. Look again." He stole a glance at Susanna Louisa, a glance that said, *Keep quiet*. To Rudi's mind, even a witch might yield to the power of suggestion. If anyone was going to utter the words "magic beans," Rudi wanted it to be the witch herself.

The witch held the beans in the dancing light of the stove's grate, causing their keyhole markings to shiver. She tilted her head and stirred the beans with a finger.

"What's this?" She pinched one between finger and thumb, held it close, and examined it. She looked up with a start. "Where did you find these?"

"At the market in Klausen," said Susanna. "We were—"

"Klausen?" The witch scowled. "Klausen is under my protection. Who dares bring these beans into my province?"

"A shearling girl gave them to us in trade," explained Susanna.

"In trade? For what?"

"For one of our cows," admitted Rudi. "And Papa is anxious to undo the bargain." Rudi suddenly decided that asking the witch for help was neither silly nor superstitious.

"Your papa is anxious over nothing," said the witch. "An entire cow for not enough beans to make a proper soup? 'Tis hardly a fair trade."

"It *is* fair!" cried Susanna. "Because they're special beans. These beans are—"

"Magic?" said the witch.

"Yes!" said Susanna Louisa.

"No!" protested Rudi. "How can they be magic?"

The witch dumped the beans back into their pouch and yanked the string tight. "I'd know that keyhole mark anywhere. These beans belongs to *him*. To the witch of Petz."

7

Petz. There were many stories about the place, and they all made Rudi shiver.

Petz was the edge of the world, or so it seemed. It was the last outpost in the mountains—a place more forbidding even than the Berg, if such a thing were possible—shrouded in cold shadow and in mystery. Travelers were obliged to journey past the province of Petz if they wanted to gain entry to the foreign lands beyond the mountains. But few people ventured so far, and Rudi knew of no one who ever ventured to Petz by choice. The place was so desolate, and so brutally exposed to the elements, that it lay encrusted in everlasting ice—ice that all but imprisoned its inhabitants. Or so the stories went.

A dozen questions swirled in Rudi's head, and he didn't know which to ask first.

Susanna Louisa had no such trouble. "There's another witch?" she blurted. "And he's a *he*?"

The old woman tossed the pouch aside. "Certainly there's another witch. There's many. One for each province of the world, I expect. As for being a *he*, why not? In Petz he's called by many names. Witch-king. Conjurer. *Hexenmeister*. Some simply calls him the Giant. Call him what you please, but he's a witch, same as me, and his realm is Petz, and his magic has no business on *my* mountain."

"I knew it," declared Susanna. "They *are* magic beans!"

Rudi's breath caught in his throat. Did Susanna Louisa have a talent for spotting magic, after all?

"They're magic, right enough." The witch scowled. "That keyhole is his mark." She slid out of her chair and began to pace the room.

Remembering that this was how the Brixen Witch preferred to do her thinking, Rudi nudged Susanna, who shifted on the rug to give the old woman room to think properly.

"His mark?" asked Susanna Louisa.

The witch waved toward the pouch on the table. "'Tis how he knows them things that hold his magic."

Rudi sat up straighter. Perhaps Susanna had a talent

for spotting magic, but Rudi had something she didn't have. He had experience. "You mark your magic too, mistress. Your magical possessions sing to you."

The old woman lifted her chin. "'Tis how a clever witch does it. How else can one know when one's magic has been stolen?" She continued her pacing.

Susanna Louisa's eyes grew wide. "That foreign girl *stole* the magic beans?"

Rudi felt a curious need to defend the red-haired shearling girl. "Perhaps she simply found them," he ventured. "Perhaps she didn't know they were magic." He pulled at his collar. "Anyone could make that mistake."

The witch raised an eyebrow at Rudi. "Accidental thievery is thievery all the same." She shook her head. "No witch gives up magic willingly. Not even that second-rate witch from Petz."

"Oh well," said Susanna brightly. "It seems the beans are yours now, mistress. I should think they'd come in handy for someone such as yourself."

The fire sputtered and waned in the grate, casting the room into shadow once more. Rudi could scarcely make out the witch's shape, but her voice was clear and cold.

"Firstly," she said, a disembodied voice in the gloom, "I does not want—nor need—extra magic. I has fared quite well these last few hundred years with the magic I has." Now the flames sprang up once more as the witch stirred the fire with a poker. "Secondly, those beans are not mine to keep. There's only so much magic in the world, and misplaced magic is trouble. Things gets thrown out of balance." She tossed the poker into the corner with a clang. "That magic does not belong in Brixen. It belongs to the witch of Petz, and I fear he may be reckless enough to come looking for it."

Rudi scratched his ear. "Why not let him come, then, and be done with it? If he's a second-rate witch, perhaps he won't cause trouble. Perhaps he'll just take his beans and go home."

The witch resumed her pacing. "Second-rate witches is the worst kind, on account of they doesn't know they're second-rate. No. Magic crossing borders is trouble enough. But a witch?" She shuddered. "'Tis strictly forbidden. Two witches in one province and none in the other? Disaster."

Rudi heard a distant rumble of thunder outside the mountain. Or perhaps the mountain itself was rumbling.

"One witch at a time," came a voice. It was Susanna Louisa.

The witch stopped midpace. "How's that?" Her eyes bore into the girl, and Rudi felt a pang of sympathy for Susanna.

But Susanna did not shrink from the witch's gaze.

"It sounds like magic has rules. And that's one of them. One witch at a time."

The witch's face crinkled, and she waggled a finger at Susanna. "Clever girl."

Rudi's mouth dropped open. He had a vague sense of feeling both pleased and unnerved at the same time. He blinked at Susanna Louisa, and then he shook himself. Susanna may have had a sudden eruption of cleverness, but he had already earned the Brixen Witch's trust and respect. Didn't that count for something?

Rudi tried to word his next question just so. "Mistress? If that's the rule—one witch at a time—then what happens when a witch . . . er . . ."

"Dies?" She spoke so quickly that Rudi wondered if she had read his mind.

Rudi gulped. "Or otherwise . . . abandons her post?"

The witch added a log to the fire. "Certainly it happens from time to time. A witch grows too old, or meets a bad end. And so another witch must come forward to take her place. But not until such time." She shut the grate and brushed her hands clean.

"Are *you* too old, mistress?" blurted Susanna Louisa.

"Ha! I'll be here another thousand years at least. And I has no plans to meet a bad end, neither."

Rudi couldn't imagine anyone ever *planning* to meet a bad end. "Where does a new witch come from?"

he asked. "Is there someone always at the ready, just in case?"

The witch settled into her chair once more and folded her hands on her chest. "'Tis usually the person who is most ready at the time. Someone with a natural gift for magic, but you both knows that's not as rare a gift as one might think." Her small eyes bore into Rudi, and then Susanna, causing them both to squirm uncomfortably. "Of course, 'tis one thing to recognize the magic in a bean, for instance, or to confer with witches. 'Tis another thing entirely to perform an enchantment of your own, or to disarm an enchantment already put forth. Skill of that kind is rare indeed. 'Tis customarily such a person who becomes a witch."

Rudi thought about this. "Could *we*—Er, could *anyone* with a gift for magic learn such skills?"

The witch raised an eyebrow. "'Tis the same as anything else, I suppose. Milking a cow. Baking elderberry tarts. Most anyone can learn such skills. But some folk learns better than other folk, through practice, or because it comes more naturally." She rummaged on her little table until she found the package of elderberry tarts. "And then, of course, such a person must be willing to take on a burden of untold immensity for uncountable years." She took a satisfied bite of tart.

"It sounds simple enough," said Susanna Louisa brightly.

Rudi stared at her. The words were simple enough, it was true. But the actual requirements seemed nearly impossible.

"'Tis a choice," said the Brixen Witch, brushing the crumbs from her lap. She snatched up the little pouch. "Now to the matter at hand. Someone must return this errant magic to Petz before it causes trouble beyond repair." She eyed Rudi up and down, as if taking the measure of him. "And now you know the rules," she said, "so you know it cannot be myself."

Rudi's stomach fluttered. "Mistress," he said, "they say that Petz is three days' journey through the mountains, at least. And that's in good weather!"

The witch waved a hand. "The nearest settlement is three days' journey, aye. But the border is an hour's climb at most. From there you can take the shortcut." She stood and laid a hand on Rudi's shoulder. "'Tis a treacherous task, young Rudolf. The choice must be yours. Still, there's no one I'd sooner send than Gussie's own grandson."

Rudi considered her words. She was counting on him. Was he not equal to the task? He would make the Brixen Witch—and Oma—proud of him. Besides, he decided, how much trouble could a second-rate witch really be?

Before he could change his mind, he lifted himself from the little stool and shook out his stiff legs. "I—

we—will go." It seemed that Susanna Louisa was meant
to accompany him on any errand the witch might have.
At any rate, he could not leave Susanna behind. Even
a witch might soon arrive at the limits of aggravation if
left alone with Susanna Louisa for very long. Nor could
he send her home alone. She would have to come with
him.

"'Tis decided, then," said the Brixen Witch, tossing
the pouch to Rudi. "Carry this infernal pile of trouble
back to where it belongs. But do it proper. Return the
beans to the Giant's lair, deep within the province of
Petz." She handed Susanna her coat. "Except for one
bean. Bury a single bean at the border—if you wants to
come home again, which I imagine you do."

"Yes," squeaked Rudi, who was beginning to wonder if he'd agreed to the errand too quickly. "What will
the bean do?"

The old woman gave Rudi his knapsack and water
skin. "The witch of Petz enchants his borders so that
no one can leave his province unless he permits it.
The magic in a single bean will be enough to break the
enchantment, at least in that place." She settled Rudi's
cap onto his head. "Even so, it's best you not let the
hexenmeister know you're visiting."

Rudi nearly tripped over his own boots. "We're
supposed to go all the way to the Giant's lair and back
again without the Giant's knowing?"

"Quite so," answered the witch, patting him on the cheek. "If you wants to come home again."

"How will we find the Giant's lair?" asked Susanna, buttoning her coat.

"You're a clever lass, are you not?" With that, the witch ushered them out the door. "Off with you now! Look for the shortcut. But mind, rules is rules. Once you cross the border, you'll be on your own. I has no power in Petz."

And then she was gone, shut again inside the mountain.

8

They stood squinting in the shade of the mountain crevice.

Rudi hitched up his pack and adjusted his cap, and they stepped into the sunshine and onto the path leading upward, toward the very peak of the Berg. He had to trust that once they reached the border, they would be able to find the shortcut.

The Brixen Witch was on their side, he reminded himself. She would not send them into Petz unless they were armed with everything they needed.

"I wasn't afeared of the witch, was I, Rudi? We had a proper conversation, didn't we?"

"Yes, Susanna," Rudi admitted. "You did very well." And despite himself, Rudi felt proud of her.

She smiled broadly. "Thank you, Rudi. I'm glad

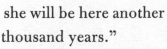

she will be here another thousand years."

"So am I," said Rudi, and he meant it.

And so they climbed. Here there was no real path to speak of—only a narrow, trickling streambed strewn with rocks. Trying not to slip, they picked their way along, climbing ever higher.

Susanna Louisa was the first to see the signpost.

"Look, Rudi!" She pointed toward a gray and weather-beaten post rising into view as they approached the peak of the mountain. Onto the post had been affixed a gray and weather-beaten plank of wood. Burned there in neat letters with a steady hand, and with an arrow pointing in the direction from which they had come, was the word BRIXEN. Beneath it, with an arrow pointing onward, black gashes spelled out PETZ.

The border.

They were standing at the very summit of the Berg. Here the ground fell away in all directions. There was nothing to break the force of the icy wind, and even the sun's warmth was swept away. In the distance lay the mountains beyond the Berg, a range of peaks Rudi had never seen. Clouds darkened the sky above the distant peaks, as if a storm were gathering but dared not breach the mountains.

The ground on the Petz side of the signpost was covered in a thick layer of ice that stopped abruptly at the border, leaving no doubt where Brixen ended and Petz began. Rudi had seen ice fields such as this before; they were a common feature of the mountain landscape. But to think that this particular body of ice seemed to know where it belonged—and where it did not—made Rudi shiver.

Or perhaps it was only the wind.

Still, one thing was abundantly clear: a single step onto the ice, and they would leave behind the province of Brixen and enter the enchanted province of Petz. And, Rudi reminded himself, they would be beyond the help of the Brixen Witch.

"I don't see any shortcut!" Susanna shouted above the wind. She stepped toward the edge of the ice.

"Wait!" Rudi flung out an arm to block Susanna's way. "The border is enchanted, remember? We have to plant a bean first." And so he took one bean from the pouch and knelt on the rocky ground beside the signpost. With his pocketknife he chipped a tiny hole at the edge of the ice. He dropped the bean snugly into the hole, where its keyhole mark stared at him like an unblinking eye. He covered the bean with a stone.

"How will we know if the bean has broken the enchantment?" said Susanna.

Rudi shrugged. They wouldn't know, he supposed, until they had stepped across the border, and then it would be too late anyway. They had to trust the Brixen Witch.

And then, despite the wind, Rudi thought he heard a muffled rumbling. A moment later, the ground beneath their feet trembled ever so slightly. The trembling continued, and grew steadily stronger, and the rumbling filled their ears.

"Rudi?" came Susanna Louisa's voice in a harsh squeak.

Now the ground shook so violently that Rudi was sure the entire mountain would crumble away beneath them. He grabbed Susanna's hand and crouched with her in the narrow space between two boulders. There was nothing he could do but squeeze his eyes shut, hold tightly to Susanna, and wait for the world to end. Silently he cursed his own foolishness. It was one thing to volunteer himself, but what choice had Susanna been given? He was responsible for her. And now he had brought her to this treacherous place at the top of the world.

Then, as quickly as it had started, the noise and shaking ceased. Even the wind quieted. They crouched for a long moment, not daring to move. Finally Rudi opened one eye, and then the other.

The world had not ended. The mountain had not gone crashing down. The signpost still loomed above their heads, pointing toward home in one direction, and in the other direction toward the frozen unknown.

But something had changed. The light seemed paler somehow, as if a cloud had passed over the sun.

Perhaps it was an illusion. Perhaps Rudi had shut his eyes too tightly for too long, and now they were playing tricks on him. Gathering his courage, he pried Susanna Louisa's arms from around his waist and peered from behind the rocks.

He gasped.

Susanna Louisa peered out too, and her mouth dropped open. "The magic, Rudi. It's happening!"

And so it was. Out of the ground had erupted a tangled green net of sturdy shoots, unfurling leaves, and twirling tendrils. Rudi watched, stunned, as tiny white flowers blossomed on the vines, and then faded and dropped, giving way to—

"Bean pods," Rudi breathed.

The vines quivered and swayed. They reached long fingers up the signpost, twisting and winding around the weathered wood until they crept across the sign itself, obliterating the word BRIXEN and all indication of home. Finally, the sheer weight of the vines cracked the post at its base. With a creaky sigh, the sign-post fell to the ground.

And still the vines grew

skyward, a dense green network of tendrils that grasped nothing but air. Soon the bean plant was wider than Rudi could spread his arms, and twice his height . . . three times his height . . . Though Rudi and Susanna stood on the very peak of the Berg, the vine grew higher, and higher still.

Rudi craned his neck and shaded his eyes, but he could not see the top of the vine.

"Look, Rudi!" said Susanna, pointing toward the broken signpost. Only the gashed word PETZ remained uncovered, and its arrow now pointed toward the sky.

Rudi and Susanna blinked at each other, and then said the word together.

"Shortcut."

9

They stood together in the stillness, heads back, mouths open, and eyes wide.

"Is it safe, Rudi?"

Rudi wondered the same thing. But before he could answer, there came a fluttering sound. Susanna ducked and covered her head, apparently expecting another upheaval of the earth. But Rudi pointed at the ice. "Look! It's only a bird."

And so it was. A snow finch, one of the tiny, fragile creatures that somehow managed to survive on the upper reaches of the mountain. With a flurry of its black-and-buff wings, it swooped up from the ice field and alighted on the vine, picking at a tender green pod.

"He's hungry, poor thing," observed Susanna as the

finch flitted among the vines. It plucked another pod and fluttered with it to the ice.

Susanna tugged at a braid. "Do you see that, Rudi? Even the birds of Petz don't dare to cross the enchanted border."

"I can't imagine a second-rate witch would concern himself with a bird," answered Rudi absently, for he had noticed something else. "Look. The vine has an opening." He stepped closer to the beanstalk. "It's really a whole network of vines, woven together into a kind of tunnel. A tunnel that goes up."

"I see it," said Susanna in wonderment. "This really is the shortcut, then? Petz is in the sky?"

Rudi reached out and tried to shake the beanstalk. It was as solid as an oak tree. "I suppose we'll find out soon enough."

And yet he could not quite bring himself to start climbing. He wished he could leave the bean pouch on the ice and return home now.

Do it proper, the Brixen Witch had told him. Rudi and Susanna would have to find the Giant's dwelling place and deliver the beans there. It would be the only way to know the magic was safely back where it belonged.

And they had to do it without the Giant's knowledge.

Rudi's thoughts were interrupted by a choked scream.

It was Susanna Louisa. She pointed at the ground, horrified. "The bird!"

With a vague sense of dread, Rudi let his gaze follow the direction of Susanna's pointing finger.

There was the snow finch, perched on the bare ground near their feet. But now it had lost all its color, and stood as still as the stones beneath it. Even the bean pod in its beak had gone white.

Rudi blinked, and blinked again. The bird did not move.

"What's happened to it?" asked Susanna in a small voice. "It looks . . . frozen."

Then the little bird, no bigger than Susanna's fist, cracked and crumbled. It shattered into a thousand bits of ice and was blown away on a gust of wind.

Rudi and Susanna stood for a long moment, unable to move or speak.

Finally, Rudi found his voice. "The border. It crossed the enchanted border into Brixen."

"I'm not going near that beanstalk," Susanna Louisa announced, taking a step backward. "I don't want to turn into a pile of ice!"

Rudi could hardly blame her. But he had made a promise to the Brixen Witch.

And the Brixen Witch had made them a promise too. Hadn't she?

"Susanna," he told her, "you don't want this stolen

magic causing trouble at home, do you? You heard the Brixen Witch. It must be done. *We* are the ones who must do it. You want her to be proud of you, don't you?"

"I won't know she's proud of me if I'm frozen!" Susanna folded her arms across her chest and took another step backward.

He tried again. "The snow finch hopped directly from the ice of Petz onto the bare ground of Brixen. As long as we cross the border by way of the vine, we'll be safe. The enchantment is broken in that place only. Just as the Brixen Witch told us. We can trust our witch, can't we? Of course we can."

Susanna pursed her lips, stomped her foot, and shook her head.

Rudi rubbed his hands on his trousers and considered their situation. There was only one thing to do.

He took a deep breath and approached the bean vine. Trying not to look at the spot where the snow finch had been, he lowered his head and stepped into the vine's doorway.

Nothing happened.

There Rudi stood, one foot on the bare ground of Brixen and one foot on the ice of Petz. All around him the vines were gloriously green and fragrant. He inhaled deeply, but he realized that his heart was pounding.

"Rudi?" came Susanna's wavering voice. "Are you all right?"

"I think so." Rudi stepped out of the tunnel of vines to stand, once again, on Brixen soil. And once again—to his great relief—nothing happened.

"You're not frozen!" declared Susanna.

With a surge of relief, Rudi let out a laugh. "We only need to keep inside the vine and we'll be safe," he said. "Ready?"

"Yes, Rudi," answered Susanna Louisa. "Now I'm ready."

And so they climbed. For this had to be what the Brixen Witch meant for them to do, as surely as if she were standing before them, pointing the way up.

The climbing was easy enough, for the vines had entwined themselves to form a ladder of sorts. The footholds were perfectly spaced, so that each rung of the ladder lay within easy reach of their next step. The vines were thick, but not so thick that their fingers couldn't grab hold. It seemed almost as if the ladder knew the size of its climbers. It grew behind them too, and on both sides, so that they were climbing in a tunnel of leaves and vines. Perhaps the Brixen Witch could not help them in Petz, but Rudi was sure that at least some of the vine's magic must be hers. She would not let them fall.

A sweet, green scent filled Rudi's nostrils as he climbed. Below him, Susanna's hair and shoulders were dusted with spent blossoms.

"See this, Rudi?" she called to him, and she held up a pod. "If I pick one that's the same size as my pinky finger, it's sweet and tender. Not smaller, because there's nothing to it. Not bigger, because then it's too tough." She popped the pod into her mouth and crunched.

"Clever girl," he muttered, echoing the witch's words. Whether he felt admiration or vexation, he wasn't sure, and he decided not to dwell on it.

Was it a good idea, eating enchanted beans? But his stomach grumbled, and his mouth watered. Bean pods sprouted all around him, tempting him as he climbed.

There's only so much magic in the world, the Brixen Witch had said.

Curious, Rudi pulled off the fattest pod he could find and split it open. With his thumb he popped out the glistening white beans and examined them.

"No keyhole markings," he called down to Susanna. "That means only the beans in the pouch are magic, then." Which meant one other thing. "We can eat these beans!"

He reached hungrily for the emerging bean pods. But they grew so quickly that he could scarcely grab a pod before it was too tough to eat. He finally learned to watch for withering blossoms. As the petals fell away, they left a tiny pod that grew before his eyes. By the time he reached out and plucked it from the vine, the bean pod had grown to just the proper size. After two or three tries he was able to time his picking perfectly, and in a few minutes both he and Susanna were able to eat as they climbed, without breaking their steady pace upward. For the first time in a long while, his stomach felt blessedly full and quiet. So full, in fact, that he decided not to eat any more, or he'd be uncomfortably sorry.

They continued for what seemed like a few minutes, or perhaps it was a few hours. The vines surrounding them tinted everything green, though when Rudi peeked between the leaves to glimpse the world beyond, he noticed no change in the sunlight. He was barely tired, and Susanna had not complained about needing to rest. They must have been climbing for only minutes, then. Though, if he were being truthful, he could only guess at the time.

"Is it true what they say about Petz?" said Susanna Louisa. "That the sun never shines there, and folk walk about with icicles hanging from their noses?"

"Whatever makes you think that?"

"I heard a story like that once."

"I think our witch would not have sent us if she thought we would come to harm," said Rudi, trying to sound convincing. "We have to trust her."

"If you say so, Rudi."

And then, instead of growing upward, the vine ladder began tilting toward horizontal, until it became a ramp of sorts, and then it was level. The tunnel of vines grew larger, so that Rudi and Susanna were able to walk side by side and upright, only brushing their heads on the nodding leaves and pods.

Now the tunnel began sloping downward. At first the slope was gradual, but then it dipped steeply, and once more Rudi and Susanna were climbing a ladder, but this time they were climbing down. Chill air pushed through the gaps in the vines, causing the leaves to curl and wilt. After a few more minutes, Rudi's breath blew out in white puffs, and his fingers grew stiff with cold.

Rudi had hoped he would be ready for whatever might come next. But now that the moment had finally come, he did not feel ready at all. The white puffs of breath came faster now, and Rudi's heart pounded in his chest.

Then, suddenly, his feet touched solid ground. Bitterly cold air blew at him with a sudden force through an opening in the vines. A doorway.

And then he was kicked in the head.

"Ouch!"

"Sorry, Rudi!" called Susanna Louisa from above. "Why did you stop?"

"Because there's no more ladder," he said, rubbing his head. "We're at . . . the end." Rudi dared not say more, for fear of frightening Susanna Louisa.

She dropped down beside him and pulled her coat tightly around her against the cold. "The end?" She peered through the doorway, and then her eyes grew wide. "The beginning, more like. We're here. We're in Petz!"

10

They stepped out from the vines and into the teeth of an icy wind. With a gasp, Susanna shrank back to the shelter of the frostbitten beanstalk. Rudi yanked his hood over his head, and his eyes watered from the sudden blast of cold. As he blinked to clear his vision, Petz took shape before him.

It looked every bit as bleak as the stories he had heard. The first thing he noticed was the color—or rather, the lack of color. Though the thaw was well under way in Brixen, spring had not yet come to Petz. Rudi wondered if spring *ever* came to Petz. The clouds looked so thick and heavy that he could not even guess the time of day. The snow-covered ground was as gray and featureless as the sky, and the barren peak that loomed above bore an unfamiliar outline. Rudi did not know its name. He only knew it was not the Berg.

Beyond a stand of wind-battered pines, Rudi made out a jumble of blocky shapes arranged in a frozen cascade along the slope. A village, such as it was. Squat dwellings of timber and stone clung to the nameless mountain like the steps of a rickety staircase; the steeply pitched roof of one house sat nearly level with the front door of the house above it. The whole collection looked as if it might slide down the mountain at the smallest sneeze.

"Rudi?" came Susanna Louisa's voice behind him. "Now what?"

Rudi wondered the same thing. He was sharply aware that, for the first time in their lives, they were standing on truly foreign soil. Despite the shortcut along the enchanted beanstalk, this was no half-day jaunt to Klausen. Never before had Rudi stood in a place where he could not see the Berg, and he didn't like it. It made him uneasy; without the Berg to establish his bearings, the entire landscape seemed somehow *wrong*. It was an unnerving reminder that they were far from home. Beyond the protection of the Brixen Witch.

Still, he would do what he must do, and return the magic beans before the witch of Petz went abroad looking for them. Rudi buttoned his coat and took Susanna's hand. "Now we find the Giant's lair, I suppose. Let's go."

But Susanna Louisa pulled back and shook her head. "How will we find the vine again when it's time to go home? How do we even know it will still be here?"

Rudi rubbed his ear and wrinkled his nose. He made up his mind to sound convincing. "Of course the vine will be here. Look, it's sturdy and strong. It's only a little frostbitten at the edges, that's all. Our witch wouldn't let us get stuck here, would she? Of course she wouldn't." He cleared his throat, which had suddenly gone dry. "See those trees, and the village beyond? We only have to remember that the vine is here, at the bottom of the village and through the trees. See? Nothing to worry about. Nothing at all." He ventured a smile.

Susanna bit her lip. She regarded the vine, and then the village. She blinked up at Rudi, and the doubt in her eyes melted into the usual expression of trust and adoration. She took his hand once more. "Let's go, then, so we can go back home."

They walked toward the village on a lane packed with a winter's worth of snow. Up the slope, past one weathered house, and then another and another. Sprigs of mistletoe were nailed to each heavy wooden door. Rudi wondered if it was meant for decoration, or for protection, or both. Shutters stood open, once brightly painted but now faded to only a suggestion of color.

Soft light glowed behind thick panes of glass. The sharp aroma of wood smoke filled the air.

Now Rudi heard voices ahead, around a bend in the lane. A lively conversation was under way, though Rudi could not make out any words. One deep voice laughed. Another, deeper voice exclaimed loudly, and the first voice laughed again.

"Those folk sound ordinary enough," Rudi said, though he remained wary.

Susanna quickened her step. "Let's go ask them where their witch lives."

"Wait!" Rudi reached out and grasped her by the elbow. He turned her to face him, and he spoke with all the authority he could muster. "We can't just barge in and announce such a thing. We're the foreigners here, remember? We must be on our guard."

She blinked up at him and nodded obediently. And now, with proper caution, they rounded the bend and continued toward the voices.

Ahead of them, in the gloom of the narrow lane, Rudi made out two large, ghostly figures. They looked like great gray bears walking upright.

Then, as Rudi and Susanna drew nearer, the ghostly figures became two men, dressed in thick coats of shearling trimmed with fur. They wore fur-lined hats pulled low and tied under their chins. The men were busy unloading bundles of kindling from a sled and stacking them next to the nearest house. Rudi loosened his grip on Susanna's hand, which meant he had been squeezing it more tightly than he'd realized.

The men's noisy unloading stopped abruptly as they noticed the two children standing before them.

"Ho now, what's this?" boomed the first man. He was the man Rudi had heard laughing. "Look here, Franz. Visitors!"

The other man pushed his hat back on his forehead and regarded Rudi and Susanna. "So they are, Ludwig." Then he squinted at them. "Are ye lost? I never have seen neither one of you before, have I?"

"No," squeaked Rudi in answer to both questions, though he could find no real reason to be worried. The two men seemed friendly enough, if perhaps a bit loud. "We've come on an errand."

"Rudi!" hissed Susanna Louisa, tugging his arm. "I don't see any icicles on their noses."

Rudi's face burned with embarrassment, but neither man seemed to have heard, much less to have taken offense. Then, deciding Susanna had raised a good point, Rudi asked, "We *are* in Petz. Aren't we?"

"Where else?" said the first man, Ludwig, who seemed ready to burst out laughing again at any moment. "What's your errand, if you don't mind my asking?"

Rudi struggled to find the proper answer. He wanted to be polite, but he still thought it wasn't a good idea to announce his intentions to the first strangers they met.

"We've come to find out where your great giant witch lives," blurted Susanna Louisa. "Do you know where that is?"

Rudi stared at her in horror.

"You want to go home, don't you?" Susanna shivered and pulled her coat tightly around her against the bitter cold.

Ludwig sputtered and choked, as if his laugh had gotten tangled on its way out. "Hold on, now," he said, shaking his head and tugging off his thick gloves. His fingers loosened the rawhide laces beneath his chin, and he pulled off his furry hat, revealing an unruly mop of thick red hair. "Now then, let's try this again with ears," he said, his voice dropping to a more normal volume. He bent down, placed his hands on his knees, and addressed Susanna Louisa. "Because it sounded to me, under my earflaps, like you said you were looking for the witch's house."

Susanna nodded.

Ludwig stood up straight, and his eyebrows disappeared under his shock of hair. "You don't say. Hear that, Franz?"

"Hear what?" said Franz from under his hat.

Ludwig waved dismissively at Franz, who returned to unloading and stacking the kindling. Ludwig's cheerful face had become solemn, and he regarded Rudi and Susanna Louisa in turn. "I can tell by your pitifully inadequate manner of dress that you're not from here."

"We've come from Brixen," offered Susanna, to Rudi's dismay.

"Brixen?" blurted Ludwig. "What sort of business would two little weeds from Brixen have with our witch?"

Rudi shifted uncomfortably. "I'd rather not say. It's bad luck to talk of such things."

Ludwig snorted. "Your bad luck is only beginning." He regarded Rudi with a squint. "Is there any way I can dissuade you from such a task?"

"No," said Rudi. "Though, truthfully, I wish you could."

"So do I," said Ludwig, and Rudi fought the urge to let him try. But they were here. They might as well finish the task they had come for.

"The witch's manor is there," said Ludwig, nodding upslope. "At the top of the village." An uneasy look passed across Ludwig's face. "At least have a meal before you go. We don't have much, but you must be dreadful starved, come all the way from Brixen." He stepped to the heavy wooden door of the house and swung it open wide. "Agatha! We have company!"

"Coming, Papa!" came a voice from inside the house.

A moment later, the voice's owner stood in the doorway. Her red hair hung loose and shining around her shoulders, and though she was no longer wearing her heavy shearling coat, Rudi knew her at once.

11

"You!" cried Susanna, pointing.

Shocked recognition flashed in the red-haired girl's face, but it disappeared just as quickly. "So I am!" she answered, lifting her chin. "I suppose you are *you*?"

Thus she managed to flummox Susanna Louisa, who stood—for once—at a loss for words.

"My daughter, Agatha," said Ludwig, who was too busy stomping the snow from his boots to notice the tense exchange.

Rudi's mind swirled with a dozen thoughts and feelings, but they were all pushed aside by one word.

Agatha.

So that was her name.

Of course the shearling girl lived in Petz, Rudi thought. It made sense. The beans had come from Petz, after all. Wouldn't their bearer have come from here too?

Remembering his manners, Rudi introduced himself and Susanna, whose mouth still hung open.

"Pleased to meet you," said Agatha lightly, as if she had never laid eyes on either of them before this moment.

But once her father pushed past them and into the house, she scowled fiercely at Rudi and Susanna, and urgently placed a finger to her lips.

Now it was Rudi's turn to be flummoxed. Why should their acquaintance be a secret? Was Agatha afraid of her father? Though Rudi had met him only a few moments before, he couldn't imagine anyone being afraid of Ludwig.

And yet Agatha's expression was so pleading that Rudi decided to play along, for now. Once again he was struck by the same curiosity he'd felt when he'd seen her in the marketplace, looking lost and anxious. This girl had caused him all manner of trouble—she was the reason he and Susanna had been compelled to venture to Petz in the first place—and yet clearly there was more going on than Rudi knew.

He wanted to find out.

At that same moment Susanna Louisa found her voice. "I know—"

Rudi elbowed her, more forcefully than he'd

intended, but it did the trick. She held her tongue once more.

"Don't stand there letting winter into the house," called Ludwig. "Come inside and warm up!"

Rudi's thoughts were crowded aside by the delicious aroma of something cooking. Before they knew it, he and Susanna were ushered into the cottage and served a small but tasty meal of mutton-bone soup, and cabbage fried in a bit of bacon fat. It was the best meal Rudi had eaten in months. He was immensely grateful, all the more because Ludwig and Agatha clearly had so little to share.

Agatha bustled from larder to table, in an effort (Rudi suspected) to keep Susanna Louisa's mouth full for as long as possible. Ludwig kept up a brisk conversation as they ate. He was hoping for a thaw, so that he might find the boot he'd lost under the snow last September. He remarked how Rudi and Susanna seemed quite ordinary, despite all the stories he'd heard about the peculiar folk of Brixen. There was only one thing Ludwig did not mention during the meal—the giant witch. And Agatha said nothing at all.

There were many questions Rudi knew he ought to ask. And yet his sharp edge of purpose had dulled along with his hunger. Petz wasn't so terribly bleak after all (now that he was warm and fed), and the people were cordial and welcoming. Why did he need to go any farther, and risk the wrath of the witch of Petz? Couldn't they just stay here awhile, and leave the beans with Agatha? She had found them in the first place. She must know where to return them to.

But Rudi knew he could not leave the beans with Agatha, any more than he could have left them at the border. He knew better than anyone else that magic half-returned is magic not returned at all. He must deliver the beans to the Giant's doorstep, as his own witch had instructed.

And yet, instead of asking the questions that ached to be asked—about the witch of Petz, or how Agatha had come to possess the magic beans, or why she was being so secretive—Rudi simply said, "Thank you for your kindness, Master Ludwig. The dinner was delicious."

"None of this 'master' nonsense, now. Call me Ludwig." His jolly mood vanished, and his eyes bore into Rudi's. "And now your stomachs are full, will you listen to reason? Don't go near the witch's fortress. Nothing good can come of it."

"I'm grateful for your concern," said Rudi, and he meant it. "But we must. Our own witch has sent us." He felt an unexpected relief at being able to speak openly of witches. Besides, Susanna had been right. The sooner they finished their errand, the sooner they could go home.

"What sort of witch sends mere children to do her bidding?" growled Ludwig.

Pride and loyalty welled up in Rudi's chest. "The Brixen Witch trusts me."

"Us," corrected Susanna Louisa. "The Brixen Witch trusts *us*."

Rudi shifted in his chair, and his face burned. But she was right.

Ludwig worked at smoothing his unruly hair. "As long as I live, I'll never understand the likes of witches. I hope your own witch has provided you with a means to get back to Brixen. Because *our* witch has long ago laid a hex on the borders of Petz."

"We know," said Susanna, her eyes wide. "If you so much as step across the border, you're turned to ice and you shatter into a thousand pieces and blow away and are never seen again."

The snow finch, Rudi recalled with a shudder.

"Quite so," said Ludwig. "You hear that, daughter? Even foreigners know how foolish it would be to try to leave Petz."

Agatha made no response, but sat demurely at the table, hands in her lap. "It's an old story," she said finally, fixing her brown eyes on Rudi. "Everyone has heard it."

"As well they should," said Ludwig, with a pointed glance at his daughter. Agatha's face remained expressionless, though she would not meet her father's gaze.

Rudi observed this tense exchange without remark, and wondered what they were really quarreling about.

Then all at once he understood.

Agatha had been to Klausen and back, hadn't she? Which meant that she had crossed the enchanted border without the aid of the magic beanstalk, and yet somehow she had not met the same fate as the snow finch. And she had done it, Rudi was sure, without telling her father.

"Don't worry," said Susanna Louisa, oblivious to the friction between father and daughter. "Our own witch helped us get here, and she will help us get home again."

"But while we're in Petz, we are on our own," Rudi added. "We must venture to the witch's lair but avoid the witch himself, if we want to go home again."

"Which we do," added Susanna Louisa.

"Of course you do," said Ludwig, his face softening. "But truly, I cannot advise you. You'd never catch me anywhere near the place."

"If you keep to the shadows, you'll manage. The Giant's eyesight is lacking, and so is his hearing." This was Agatha, who still would not look at her father as she spoke.

"He doesn't sound very worrisome, for a witch," said Susanna hopefully.

"He makes up for it in other ways," answered Ludwig, still frowning at his daughter. "They say he can smell a drop of blood a mile away."

"Pardon me," said Rudi. "Why do you call your witch 'the Giant'?"

"He's a great huge man," answered Ludwig. "As tall as three men, with legs like tree trunks. Some say he was born that way. Others say he grows year by year."

"He's an evil tyrant," said Agatha, and now her eyes gleamed in anger. "Whatever he can, he takes for himself, and all the better if it makes us suffer. Every scrap of firewood thicker than my finger. Every scrawny rabbit we manage to snare. If anyone in Petz so much as sprouts a turnip seed on their windowsill, *he* takes it."

"So he does," said Ludwig sadly. "He made off with every cow and chicken and goat long ago. Some folk say he's hoarded the summer itself, to better control all its bounty. Then he doles it out as he sees fit. Without the meager sustenance he provides, every last one of us would freeze to death, or starve. We're forever on the brink of both at any rate. Never mind that we are prisoners in our own country."

Rudi considered all this. How lucky were the folk of Brixen that they could trust their witch, and that she treated them with fairness and respect? She was powerful enough that—if she wanted to—she could be as merciless as the witch of Petz.

"Listen to me now," continued Ludwig. "About this errand of yours. You may think you have everything in hand, but—"

A sudden scrape of chair legs, and Agatha stood. "I will show you the way."

12

They stared at her, all three of them.

Ludwig was the first to find his voice. "You will not! I just got you back from who-knows-where. I'll not risk losing you again!"

Rudi's ears perked up at this. So Ludwig knew that Agatha had been gone. But he was not sure *where* she had gone, and now Rudi was certain that Agatha did not want her father to know.

"You heard what he said, Papa. He cannot disobey his witch."

Ludwig rose from his chair, fists clenched at his sides. "But you have no such duty. You're my daughter, and you'll stay home, where you belong!"

Agatha gestured toward Rudi and Susanna. "These two are strangers here. You know they will fail miserably without someone to guide them."

Rudi managed to feel grateful and insulted all at the same time.

"Daughter!" said Ludwig, drawing himself up to his full height, which was considerable. "I'll not tell you again. You'll stay home, where you can't get into any more trouble!" With that, he tossed Rudi and Susanna their coats and knapsack, and bundled them outside. Standing with them on the doorstep, he shut the door and rubbed his arms against the cold.

"Excuse my daughter. I don't know what's come over her. For three days she was gone, without a word. Drove me nearly mad with distress and worry. I feared the worst—that she'd tried to escape across the border. That I'd never see her again. When she finally came home, just today, I was relieved beyond words. But you heard her in there. I think she ventured up to the Giant's fortress." Ludwig shivered, and shifted from one foot to the other to keep warm. "And that worries me nearly as much."

"Why did she do that?" asked Susanna, and Rudi wondered the same thing. But it would explain how Agatha had come to possess the magic beans.

Ludwig adjusted the hood on Susanna's coat. "She hates the Giant, as do we all. But I think she hates it even more that no one dares to defy him." He shook his head sadly. "I fear it will cost her dearly one day."

Ludwig's face clouded. "As for yourselves, don't make the same mistake. Listen to what I'm saying. You have been charged with an impossible task. Go home to Brixen, while you can. *If* you can."

Rudi swallowed the lump in his throat. "Truly, I wish we could." He pulled up his own hood and studied Ludwig's worried face. Though he had only just met Ludwig and Agatha, Rudi was already fond of them both. He didn't want to betray Agatha's secret. But Ludwig had been generous and kind, and didn't deserve to suffer needless worry.

And so Rudi ventured a suggestion. "Perhaps Agatha *should* come with us, then. We could help each other. She can help us avoid the Giant, and we can make sure she doesn't do anything reckless. We can make sure she gets home to you safely."

Ludwig considered this for a moment. "I don't think I can stop her, in any case. You might as well have each other to look after." He pulled out a huge handkerchief and blew his nose. "There's no sense putting it off any longer, I suppose. Are you ready?"

"We didn't bring any mittens," said Susanna in a small voice.

She was right. When they'd left home this morning, they'd never imagined they'd be going all the way to Petz.

Ludwig gave a weak smile. "Wait here." He

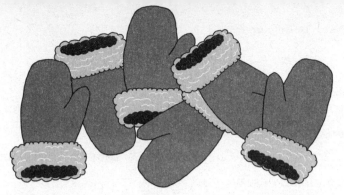

disappeared inside the house for a moment, and then returned with his arms full. He handed them pairs of shearling mittens, which were too big for Susanna Louisa, but she pulled them on without remark. Now Ludwig tied Susanna's hood snug under her chin. For good measure, he wrapped a woolen scarf several times around her neck. He offered his fur-lined hat to Rudi, who took it with a surge of gratitude, for the cold was already making his ears ache.

"Bring them back to us," Ludwig told them. "And tell us how you fared with our *hexenmeister*."

Now the cottage door opened and Agatha appeared in the doorway, bundled in her own shearling coat and hood.

Ludwig busied himself inspecting Rudi and Susanna, and then nodded in grim satisfaction. "I ought to be the one going with you, but I'm not so nimble anymore. Besides, I've seen too much of the world to be brave enough for such a task." He turned and shook a thick finger at his daughter. "If you're not home again soon, that Giant will deal with the likes of me, witch or no witch!"

"I'm very glad of it," said Agatha, and she threw her arms around her father's neck. They stood for a moment wrapped in a fierce embrace.

"Could I have one of those?" came a small voice. Susanna Louisa's.

Ludwig's pained face crinkled into a smile, and he hugged Susanna, too. "You'll be back again before you know it."

Perhaps it was Ludwig's great size, or Agatha's testy, tearful mood, or both, but to Rudi's mind, Susanna Louisa looked suddenly very small. Too small to be venturing so far from home.

And he was responsible for her.

Time to accomplish the task at hand. *Do it right*, Rudi told himself, *so you only need to do it once.* He shook Ludwig's hand without a word, lest his voice waver and betray his own fears. Ludwig gestured up the hill toward their destination and stood on the doorstep, his jaw set and his arms folded tightly across his chest.

There was nothing to do but set off. Rudi, Susanna, and Agatha trooped up the snowy lane in uneasy silence, past weather-beaten houses optimistically adorned with mistletoe. Rudi glanced over his shoulder. Ludwig still stood on the doorstep, watching them, his thick shock of hair a bright daub against the gray house. He was too far away now for Rudi to see the expression on his face, and Rudi was grateful. It made the leaving easier.

No wonder Agatha charged ahead, never once looking back at her father.

Rudi thought of his own parents. They were sharply aware of the benefits to be gained by Rudi's acquaintance with the Brixen Witch. And yet, Rudi knew that if it were up to them, Mama and Papa would never allow Rudi to have dealings with their own witch, much less the witch of Petz.

But it was not up to them. And it seemed the same was true for Ludwig and Agatha.

The three travelers continued up through the village, which looked to be held together by ice and pure luck. Small children tumbled past, as round as snowballs in their layers of warm clothing. A thick-coated dog trotted up to greet Agatha and sniff the newcomers. A bundled woman pulled frozen shirts and trousers off her wash line, stacked them like kindling, and carried the stiff pile into her crooked house.

Once again, Rudi was struck by how familiar it all seemed. Except for the outward details—the decoration on the houses; the stubborn winter; and, not least, the outline of the peak that loomed above—daily life in Petz seemed very much like daily life at home in Brixen.

"The folk of Petz seem content enough," he remarked. "Considering your giant witch is such a tyrant."

"What choice do they have?" snapped Agatha.

"They make the best of a bad situation."

As if to prove her point, a scrawny tabby cat came padding from behind a splintered shed. She mewed and wound herself around Agatha's boots.

"Pretty kitty!" said Susanna, reaching for the cat.

An exposed claw shot out and raked a deep scratch across Susanna's borrowed shearling mitten.

"Bad kitty!" Susanna cried, jumping back to hide behind Rudi. "Why does she like you and not me? Is she yours?" For the cat had resumed rubbing against Agatha's ankles, and now it was purring loudly.

"Shoo!" said Agatha, shaking her foot. "Not mine. She lives under the shed."

Rudi knew a thing or two about bad-tempered cats. His own barn cat, Zick-Zack, had not allowed anyone to touch her since she was a kitten. Now Rudi stomped his foot and said, "BOO!"

The cat arched her back, hissed, and shot under the shed.

"I seem to have a way with cats," said Agatha. "I don't know why. You'd think I had a fish in my pocket."

This caused Susanna to blink in recollection. She reached into her own coat. "I have beans in my pocket. Want one?" She popped a tiny pod into her mouth and crunched.

Agatha gasped in horror.

"Don't worry," said Susanna, opening another pod to display its contents. "They're not the magic ones. See? No keyhole mark."

Rudi winced at the mention of magic. Such talk might be commonplace here in Petz, but he was from Brixen. And in Brixen it was bad luck to talk of such things.

Agatha narrowed her eyes. "I suppose that's how you got here? You climbed the beanstalk?"

Rudi nodded, but then he frowned in puzzlement. "You too?"

"How else could I have traveled all the way back from Brixen so quickly?"

"Not Brixen," corrected Susanna, still munching. "We saw you in Klausen."

"Brixen, Klausen," said Agatha with a wave of her hand. "All the villages on the far side of the mountain are the same to me."

Rudi took notice of this remark. To him, the villages were as different as night and day. But they were foreign places to Agatha, and so he held his tongue. Still, something about her words nagged at the back of his mind.

"We never saw you," said Susanna. "Or heard you. On the beanstalk, I mean."

They had left the village behind and now were climbing through a scrubby, sparse woodland. Agatha took Susanna's hand and pulled her up the snowy slope. "I didn't see you, either. And yet here we are. Does it really matter how we got here?"

"No," said Susanna Louisa.

Yes, thought Rudi. Once again, something nagged at his mind. It was like trying to catch a tiny fish with his bare hands. The silvery thought kept flitting through his fingers. He rubbed his neck. He didn't want to upset Agatha further, but there were things he needed to know. "About those beans . . . the ones you gave to Susanna . . ."

"Those beans!" Agatha turned on Rudi. "I wish you would stop talking about those beans! The only thing worse would be if you told me you'd brought them with you back to Petz."

13

"**Oops,**" **said Susanna,** skidding to a stop on the icy path. "Then I suppose it's worse."

Agatha dropped Susanna's hand and stared at her, aghast. "I should have guessed," she said, almost to herself. "Why else would you have come all the way to Petz? You mean to return the beans to the Giant, don't you? That's your errand?"

Rudi hesitated. How easy it would be to say no. One simple word, and he could melt Agatha's anguish and see her smile. He could drop the beans where he stood, and be finished with them forever. He and Susanna could go home. One simple word.

But something happened to the word as it formed on his tongue, and it came out a wobbly but unmistakable "Yes."

Agatha's face became as pale as the sky. "But you can't! Do you know what I've endured because of those beans? He came storming after me, vowing to spill the blood of whoever stole his magic. I barely escaped with my life! And then I got lost. For three days and nights I wandered in the mountains. I worried poor Papa half to death! It was only luck that led me to the valley, and to the village."

Rudi's mouth fell open. "That's how you came to Klausen?" He recalled seeing her in the marketplace. Her tangled hair. Her muddied boots. And then he thought of the snow finch. "But the hex on the border . . ."

Agatha groaned in frustration. "There is no hex on the border! It's nothing but a fairy tale, to frighten us. To keep us from leaving."

Rudi blinked at her. He had seen for himself that the enchanted border was distressingly real. His heart sank as he realized that Agatha could not be telling the truth.

But he held his tongue. It was possible she had a good reason. Wasn't it?

Agatha continued. "I didn't know the beans were magic when I took them. Everything happened so quickly . . ."

"Why did you go up to the Giant's lair in the first place?" said Rudi, trying to contain his anger and disappointment. "You knew it was risky. That's why you didn't tell your papa." He remembered with a pang of heartache the anguish on Ludwig's face and in his voice.

"He would only have worried," said Agatha. "He believes all the stories. But I walked right through the Giant's gate, as if he were expecting me." She glanced around quickly, to be sure they were alone. "Some of the stories are true, though. Most especially, *one* story is true." Her eyes gleamed with excitement. "The story about the summer."

Rudi recalled what Ludwig had said about the Giant stealing the summer. At the time, he had barely paid attention. He'd assumed it was nothing more than Petz folklore. A story to explain away the injustice of life in a harsh place. But Rudi didn't know what to believe anymore. "You mean to say the Giant stole the summer." It was more a challenge than a question.

Agatha nodded eagerly. "Yes! But no one has dared go near his fortress in years and years. They're all afraid of him, even Papa."

"Aren't you afraid too?" said Susanna, wiping her nose with a borrowed mitten.

"I'm more afraid of living in this hopeless place forever. I ventured to the Giant's fortress to prove it could be done. And I was right! And I discovered wondrous things! Warmth and sunshine. A storehouse full of food. Whole sacks of beans! But they had such odd markings."

"The keyhole," said Susanna, nodding solemnly.

"Yes!" said Agatha. "I picked up a handful of beans.

I only meant to have a closer look. But then I heard someone coming, and his voice was like thunder. 'Trespasser! Thief! Who dares to steal my magic?' I forgot I had the beans in my hand until I was halfway home." She stopped to catch her breath, which hung about her face in an icy cloud. "And then of course I couldn't go home. I couldn't endanger Papa. . . ."

"You could have dropped the beans," suggested Rudi, because that's what he would have done.

"I nearly did," said Agatha. "But then I realized I had a weapon in my hand."

"The beans?" said Susanna, perplexed.

"The *magic*," corrected Agatha. "I realized that by taking the Giant's magic, I was taking his power. It might be a way to get back what is rightfully ours."

"But the magic is no use to you," said Rudi, who had learned a thing or two about witches. "Besides, the beans you took must be only a tiny portion of all his magic."

Agatha would not be discouraged. "Any amount of magic holds power, yes? Perhaps we don't know how to use the magic. But if it's hidden from the Giant, *he* cannot use it either."

"So you fled through the mountains," said Rudi. "And hid the beans in Klausen." Once more the image of the snow finch flitted stubbornly across Rudi's memory.

Agatha nodded. "Getting lost was a blessing in

disguise! The Giant would never follow me to another province. He thinks we all believe the story about the hex on the border." She lifted her chin in pride, and Rudi bit back the urge to tell her about the snow finch. But he decided to bide his time.

"And then," said Agatha, "I happened upon the market. I thought that if I could trade the beans to someone else, they might be carried away even farther. To someplace he'd *never* find them."

"To Brixen," muttered Rudi.

Agatha seemed not to hear. "And by then I was quite hungry anyway, and so I had another reason to make a trade. So you see? I told you I was not begging. But please—do you understand now what I've risked? I cannot let you return those beans!"

Susanna Louisa threw her arms around Agatha's waist. "Don't worry! We would never let you come to any harm."

Rudi kicked in frustration at the frozen ground. He wished it were that simple. But it seemed Agatha would come to harm whether the beans were returned or not. "The Brixen Witch has given us a task, and we are sworn to carry it out. The magic of Petz must be returned to its rightful owner. No matter that its rightful owner is a tyrant and a bully. I'm truly sorry about that part."

Agatha squinted at him. "Why must you? Aside from promising a witch, that is?"

Rudi tried again. "It's hard to explain, but it has to do with magic crossing borders. Terrible things can happen. Worse things, even, than Petz is already suffering. You must believe me. I wish we could do something to help."

Agatha stared at him in icy silence. Then finally, "A witch told you all this?"

"Yes."

"Well, then," said Agatha brightly, "there's one thing I know about witches. Not a single one of them can be trusted. You want to help me? Then come with me to the Giant's fortress, but not to return the beans. To help me steal something else. Something even more valuable than magic beans." Without waiting for an answer, she took Susanna's eager hand and started up the hill once more.

Rudi scrambled to follow. He could not do what Agatha asked, but at least they were moving again. "I promised Ludwig you'd stay out of trouble," he called after her. "Besides, you're wrong about witches. About the Brixen Witch, anyway. She's wise, and kind, and—"

"She can be testy sometimes," added Susanna Louisa helpfully. "But Rudi's right. She would never let any harm come to us. Rudi!" She turned back to face him. "Don't you think the Brixen Witch could help Agatha deal with their nasty mean giant witch? I should think she'd be very glad to help!"

"The Brixen Witch has no power in Petz," Rudi answered automatically. It was not something he wanted to say. But it was the truth.

Susanna wrinkled her brow. "What should we do, Rudi?"

Rudi thought about it. "There's more to the Brixen Witch than magic," he said finally, and that was the truth too. It gave him an idea. Before he could change his mind, he said to Agatha, "We will make a bargain with you. We will take you to ask the Brixen Witch for help . . . *after* we return the Giant's beans."

Agatha's dark eyes met his. A few strands of copper-colored hair had escaped from under her hood, and Rudi noticed how the sunlight, weak as it was, caused the strands to glow like wisps of flame around her face. She looked at Rudi sidelong. "Do you really think your witch could help me?"

Rudi hesitated. This time, more than anything, he wanted to tell her *yes*. If anyone could help Agatha, it was the Brixen Witch.

Unless, of course, no one could help Agatha.

"I'm certain of it," he said.

Agatha nodded decisively. "It's a bargain, then. I'll help *you* return those infernal beans, and your witch will help *me* steal the summer back from the Giant."

14

They continued up the slope, through a bleak and barren landscape of gray snowfields scattered with slabs of black rock and bent fir trees. The wind blew colder here, with fewer structures to block its path. Rudi pulled his borrowed hat lower on his head and silently thanked Ludwig for his kindness.

And he silently scolded himself for making his own task even harder. What had he gotten himself into just now? When he'd offered to help, he'd imagined the Brixen Witch could give Agatha a bit of practical advice. Suggestions for dealing with second-rate witches, perhaps. But stealing back the summer? Even if such a thing were within the Brixen Witch's power, would she be willing to help? Rudi had no idea how he would honor the bargain he'd just made with Agatha.

No matter, he told himself. First things first. Return the beans to the Giant's fortress, and then puzzle out what comes next.

After what seemed like hours, they approached a ridge. At least Rudi thought it must be a ridge, for as they walked, there seemed to be more sky and less ground ahead of them. Though, in truth, it was hard to tell where one ended and the other began.

As they drew nearer, the ridge took on a distinct shape. It looked like a structure of some sort, as gray as the mountain, as gray as the sky. But it was not the mountain, and it was not the sky. It was a wall of rough, sharp stone topped with a row of iron spikes. At either end of the wall, the ridge snaked away into the distance like the spine of a great gray beast. With every step the wall loomed higher.

The Giant's fortress.

Though he hadn't thought he could feel any colder, the sight of it caused Rudi to shiver. But it also filled him with a steely resolve. Their destination was finally in sight. Time to finish their task so they could go home.

"I don't like it here," declared Susanna Louisa, her words nearly blowing away on the gusting wind. "Is this a good idea, Rudi? Can't we leave the beans and go?" She sniffed deeply and wiped her dripping nose.

Rudi did not answer her. He stood, wiggling his

freezing toes inside his boots, and waited until she had finished her silent argument with herself.

Finally, Susanna wiped her nose once more and slipped her soggy mitten into his. "If you say so, Rudi. But I still don't like it here."

"This way," said Agatha.

She led them around the fortress and to the very edge of the ridge. Here the wall of the fortress turned and rose up as if it were a part of the ridge, forming a sheer cliff of stacked stone. Rudi peered around the wall, stretching himself as far as he dared against the onslaught of wind and cloud. They could go no farther unless they climbed the wall itself or stepped off the ridge into the bottomless sky.

Once more Rudi shivered. "Now what?"

"There," said Agatha, pointing. Embedded in the stone wall was a small wooden door, so badly scoured by wind and sun and sleet that it had faded to the color of the surrounding stone.

"An invisible door," said Rudi, though it was not truly invisible, now that he paid closer attention.

Agatha stepped toward the door at the edge of the mountain.

Susanna Louisa covered her eyes.

"Careful!" called Rudi.

Agatha answered by waving them closer.

But Susanna would not step closer. She gripped

Rudi's hand so tightly that when he pulled out of her grasp, he left his mitten behind.

"Ready?" said Agatha as together they stood at the door.

"Not really," admitted Rudi. "But go ahead."

With a knowing nod, Agatha reached for the iron latch and pushed the door.

Nothing happened.

She jiggled it. "The latch is stuck."

Rudi stepped forward and tried. "It's not stuck. It's locked."

Agatha groaned. "He must have locked it after I was here last time." Because everyone, even a witch, remembers to lock the door after the thief has come and gone.

Rudi stooped to peer through the iron-rimmed keyhole above the latch, and gasped at what he saw. "Is that what I think it is?"

"Yes," said Agatha, her eyes gleaming.

"What's going on?" This was Susanna Louisa, curiosity overcoming her fear.

Rudi pointed, and Susanna peeked through the keyhole. "I can't see a thing. There's something green in the way." Rudi waited for Susanna's brain to catch up with her eyes. Finally: "Agatha! It's your summer!" Susanna rattled the door handle. "It's locked! Now what?"

Rudi did not remark on how quickly Susanna's

courage had returned, even while his was waning again. He only sighed and shook his head.

Then he remembered something. "Marco the blacksmith gave me a key."

"He did?" said Susanna. "When?"

"Just before we left Brixen. A skeleton key. He said it would open all but the most devious lock." Rudi pulled off his remaining mitten and searched the pockets of his coat. Finally he found it, heavy and large and warm. With his companions hovering around him, Rudi drew a breath and inserted the key into the lock.

It would not turn.

"Let me try," said Susanna, pushing forward and jiggling the key. She frowned. "It won't turn."

"I know that!" said Rudi. "You said the key would work in any lock!"

"Any but the most devious lock," corrected Agatha. "What could be more devious than the locked fortress of a devious witch?" She held out her gloved hand, and Susanna obediently laid the key upon it. "And what better way to enter the devious witch's locked fortress than with his own magic?" She held out her other hand. "The keyhole beans."

Rudi took a halting step backward. "I don't think it's safe for anyone but a witch to use magic."

Agatha shrugged. "One way to find out, yes?" She

stared at him with hand outstretched, waiting.

But Rudi stood his ground. "We need to take the beans inside and put them back where you found them. We made a bargain."

Agatha persisted. "I only want to borrow one bean. I'll give it back. You want to get inside, don't you?"

Rudi squinted at her. "How do you know it will work?"

"How do you know it won't?"

He sighed in exasperation. It reminded him of his arguments with Oma. Arguments he always lost.

And so Rudi struggled with the buttons of his coat, until finally he was able to reach into his trouser pocket for the little pouch of beans. As he drew it out, it was caught by the wind. Susanna gasped, and Rudi tightened his grip on the strings. One careless gesture, and the magic beans would slip from his stiff fingers and sail away into the cloud and fog, to be lost forever. He shuddered at the thought.

Turning his back to the rim of the ridge, he pulled carefully at the strings of the pouch, reached inside, and drew out a single white bean. Its keyhole mark glinted darkly in the gray light.

"Be careful," he said again as he handed it to Agatha. He sounded embarrassingly like his mother, but just now he didn't care.

With a satisfied grin, Agatha took the bean and

promptly pushed it into the keyhole of the wooden door.

"Now what?" said Susanna, leaning closer to inspect the result.

"Now the key." Once more, Agatha inserted the heavy iron key into the lock. Rudi held his breath.

This time the key turned with a loud *click*. The door swung open.

15

And so they stood at the entrance to the Giant's fortress.

Behind them the icy wind wailed, unabated. Before them lay a calm green meadow full of wildflowers and droning honeybees. A tall hedge, studded with bramble and wild roses, followed the inner course of the wall. A distant hillside was dotted with sheep. And in the center of it all stood a grand house, built of the gray stone of the mountain.

A blessedly warm breeze bathed Rudi's frostbitten face, but his feet refused to carry him into the fortress. "How did you do that?"

Agatha shrugged. "The Giant's lock. The Giant's magic bean. It makes sense, yes?" She stooped to retrieve the bean from the ground and handed it to Rudi, who hurried to return it to the safety of the pouch.

"Look, Rudi! Lambs!" Susanna pushed past him through the doorway and into summer in full flower.

Into the realm of the *hexenmeister*.

Rudi knew he must follow her, but still he hesitated. It was one thing to venture into a foreign witch's province. It was another thing to trespass in a witch's own backyard.

At that moment, a freezing gust pushed at Rudi's back and slipped its icy fingers down his neck. With a shudder, Rudi lurched across the threshold and into the midst of enchanted summer.

The sweet soft air covered him like a blanket. He inhaled deeply the scent of musky hedge roses and freshly mown hay. He lifted his face to the sun and pulled off his fur hat to feel the warmth on his bare head. "So the story is true," he said.

"I told you," said Agatha, shutting the door behind her and erasing all sign of winter. "Don't worry. It opens again, see?" She demonstrated, and Rudi let out a breath he hadn't realized he'd been holding.

Susanna fluttered over to them. "The flowers smell lovely, Rudi. The grass is so green and soft. How can such a beautiful place be home to such an awful witch?" She unwrapped her borrowed woolen scarf and unbuttoned her coat.

Rudi glanced around, half-expecting something—or

someone—to swoop down upon them. "We must be careful."

Agatha plucked a pink rosebud, closed her eyes, and inhaled its scent. Pocketing the rosebud, she gave a nod toward the manor. "The storehouse is around back. Stay behind the hedge, where he can't see us."

And so she led them single file along the narrow space between the hedge and the wall, where they could remain concealed from watchful eyes. Through the hedge Rudi caught occasional glimpses of the Giant's house.

"I hear the lambs, Rudi," said Susanna in a loud whisper. "And cows! Don't you wish we could take a cow home to Brixen? Why does one person own so much? Even if he is a witch? Why does he get a beautiful house when our dear little witch gets only a cave inside a mountain?"

Rudi wished he knew the answers to her questions. He wished he could demonstrate a superior knowledge of witches. But he could only shrug. "Perhaps our witch prefers humble things."

"I cannot imagine any witch being humble about anything," Agatha whispered over her shoulder. "It would be like a snake that doesn't slither."

Despite Agatha's confidence, Rudi's uneasy feeling would not subside. But there was no movement except for birds rustling in the hedge; no sound except the buzzing of honeybees and the distant bawling of sheep. Rudi wondered how the witch of Petz had managed to steal the summer. Perhaps it was all an illusion. An enchantment, meant to lure unsuspecting trespassers into the witch's lair, like so many moths to a web. Whatever it was, it didn't seem like the work of a second-rate witch.

"Listen," said Rudi. "If the Giant shows himself before we get to the storehouse, we should drop the beans and run. It's not the best thing, but it might have to do."

"If the Giant shows himself, we're done for anyway," said Agatha. "So I suggest we don't rouse him in the first place."

After a few minutes' wary walking, they had rounded the manor house and now were standing within sight of its back garden. They dashed across a small expanse of open meadow toward another stone wall, this one only as high as Rudi's waist. The wall enclosed a cobbled yard with a chicken coop and a kitchen garden full of fragrant herbs. The front of the house had been regal and imposing. But here, in the back, it was homey. Welcoming. Rudi almost wished he could sit on the wall and bask in the sunlight.

"There's the storehouse," whispered Agatha, indicating a small stone outbuilding at the far end of the wall. "The door is on the other side."

Rudi nudged Susanna Louisa, who was gazing

dreamily at the hens scratching in the yard. "Listen, Susanna, we should stay together. We'll return the beans and then go."

She nodded, but she was watching the chickens so intently that Rudi wondered if she had heard him. He grasped her by the arm. "We're ready, Agatha."

With one last glance toward the manor house, Agatha pushed away from the wall and dashed toward the storehouse.

Before Rudi could follow, Susanna gasped. Her mouth hung open, and she pointed at the courtyard.

Rudi froze. "What's wrong?"

"There!" cried Susanna, forgetting all about being quiet. "Hildy!"

"Where? Who?" And then he remembered. Hildy was Susanna Louisa's pet hen.

"That's impossible, Susanna. Hildy is back home in Brixen."

"No! That's her!" And Susanna Louisa scrambled to climb the low wall.

"Rudi!" said Agatha from the other direction. "Are you coming?"

Rudi felt the blood drain from his head. He had no choice. He was responsible for Susanna Louisa. He could not let her be seized by the Giant because of a familiar-looking chicken.

"Wait!" he called to Agatha. He fumbled in his

pocket, and then finally drew out the little pouch and tossed it to her. In a single motion she caught the pouch, turned, and bolted toward the storehouse.

Susanna had managed to climb onto the wall, and now she stood with a full view of the courtyard. And the chickens had a full view of her. They scurried and squawked, and Rudi would have shushed them if he'd thought it would do any good.

"Hildy!" called Susanna. "Come here!"

Rudi frantically tugged at Susanna's ankle. "I don't think chickens come when you call them."

"Of course they don't. You have to go get her."

"Don't be silly, Susanna! That hen only looks like Hildy."

"That *is* her! I'd know her speckles anywhere. Besides, I can prove it. She has a scar on her leg. She got it in a fight with a mean rooster. And I rescued her, and now she's my very own hen, and that nasty *hexenmeister* can't have her!"

Several thoughts swirled in Rudi's head. But the first thing he blurted was, "*You* rescued Hildy from a rooster? How?"

"Easy. I stood in the yard and screamed until Papa came running and separated them with a rake."

"Oh."

"And ever since, Hildy is my very own hen. I'd know her anywhere. How did she get to Petz? We need to take her home! Please, Rudi. We can't leave Hildy here!"

Rudi winced. Despite his better judgment, something told him they would not be leaving without this hen. And something *else* told him that because of the racket they were making, they might have company very soon. He glanced toward the storehouse, but there was no sign yet of Agatha. How long could it take to toss a handful of beans into the proper sack?

"Hildy!" Susanna called again. "Come here now!"

Before he could change his mind, Rudi climbed onto the low stone wall. He kept one eye on the storehouse and one eye on the speckled hen, who fluttered toward him just inside the wall. As soon as Hildy passed him, Rudi leaped down and gave chase. Susanna jumped in front of Hildy to block her path. In the confusion, the hen flapped into a corner of the yard. Seeing his chance—perhaps his only chance—Rudi dove onto the cobbles and wrapped his arms around Hildy.

Hildy squawked wildly and pecked the air. She kicked her legs, and tried to flap her wings, but Rudi held on tight.

"Here, Rudi!" It was Agatha, appearing out of nowhere and offering an empty burlap sack.

In a flurry of speckled feathers, Rudi grabbed the sack and stuffed Hildy in.

"We did it!" Susanna threw her arms around Agatha. "Hildy! You're saved!"

Inside the sack, Hildy gave one last halfhearted flutter, as if already accepting her fate. The other chickens, apparently relieved that the attention had not been directed at them, went back to their clucking and scratching. Rudi sat sprawled on the cobbles, breathless and hot. He had torn his pants and bruised his knee. His knuckle was bleeding.

"Thank you, Rudi!" whispered Susanna Louisa, as if whispering mattered now.

Rudi brushed the dust out of his hair with one hand, and sucked on the bloody knuckle of the other.

Agatha helped him to his feet. "We should go. Now."

"The beans," he gasped. "Did you—"

But his words were interrupted by a sound. It started low and far away.

Fummm.

Susanna's eyes grew wide. "Rudi? What was that?"

Rudi swallowed a lump the size of a hen's egg. "I'm not sure. . . ."

"It's time to go," said Agatha grimly, and she vaulted over the stone wall.

Fummm. . . . Fummm. The low sound was louder now, and closer. Rudi wasn't sure if he heard it with his ears or felt it with his body, or both. He grabbed Susanna and heaved her over the wall into Agatha's arms.

Fummm. . . . Fummm. . . . FUMMM.

"Rudi! Hurry!" Susanna yelped.

Rudi hoisted the squawking sack onto his shoulder and scrambled over the wall.

FUMMM. . . .

The sound was coming from inside the manor house. And it was most definitely getting closer. Agatha was already sprinting for the hedge.

Rudi grabbed Susanna's hand. "Run!"

16

Rudi and Susanna raced across the meadow after Agatha. If they could reach the shelter of the hedge before the Giant caught sight of them, they might have a chance to escape.

FUMMM. . . .

They dived through an opening in the hedge just as new sounds came to Rudi's ears. A door slamming. A voice bellowing in the open air. "Who dares to invade my home? Where is the thief whose blood is spilled on my doorstep?"

Rudi's breath caught in his throat. His scraped knuckle stung and throbbed, but it hardly bled at all.

So that story is true too, Rudi thought.

He sprinted along the narrow pathway between the hedge and the wall. He could barely keep Agatha in sight ahead of him, but he dared not let go of Susanna's hand. And the chicken was heavy, and the sack bounced on his shoulder and kept catching on the brambles in the hedge.

FUMMM. . . .

Just when Rudi thought he might collapse from effort, the small wooden door came into view. Agatha was already there, struggling with the latch. As Rudi and Susanna caught up with her, the latch gave way and Agatha wrenched the door open. She pushed Rudi and Susanna through and then followed them out, slamming the door behind her and plunging them into winter once more.

The cold air slapped Rudi's face like an icy hand. He gasped and coughed as the cold filled his lungs. He buttoned his coat as best he could.

"To the beanstalk!" Agatha shouted over the howling wind.

"But your papa!" said Susanna. "He's waiting for us! We promised him!"

Agatha shook her head. "That's the first place the Giant will look. He will kill us if he finds us, and Papa, too!" She grabbed Susanna's hand and started across the slope.

"Wait!" Rudi remembered exactly where the beanstalk stood. Down the slope, past the village, behind a clump of trees. He had committed it to memory for just this circumstance. "This way!" He pulled Susanna in the opposite direction.

"Don't be silly!" said Agatha, pulling even harder, until Rudi thought poor Susanna might be torn in two.

FUM. . . .

There was no time to argue. This was Agatha's mountain. Perhaps she knew a shortcut. Or a roundabout way, so as not to lead the Giant through the village and past her father's house.

FUM. . . .

Rudi had no choice. He followed Agatha.

They hurried across the slope, in the opposite direction from the way they had come. In a moment another hedge came into view, half-hidden in the icy fog.

But it was not a hedge. It was the beanstalk, and it was nowhere near the place where Rudi had thought it would be. How had be become so disoriented? But after the horrible confusion of the last few moments, he did not care. He followed Agatha and Susanna into the vines of the beanstalk, and began to climb upward inside the green tunnel.

"Will the Giant follow us?" said Susanna, and Rudi stole a fearful glance below him. He was wondering the same thing.

"I hope not," said Agatha. "He's not very fast. And I don't think he'd fit."

Rudi found no comfort in this. But as they climbed ever higher, all was quiet below them.

Before long the beanstalk began to level out, and just as before, it soon became a tunneled roadway. They were able to move more quickly here, and Rudi adjusted the burlap sack on his shoulder. Hildy did not protest but only clucked uncertainly, as if she knew there was nothing she could do about her situation. Rudi knew how she felt.

"Rudi?" said Susanna after a few moments. "How do you suppose Hildy got to Petz? Has the Giant been to Brixen?"

Rudi's mouth went dry at the thought. The Brixen Witch had warned about the danger of witches crossing borders. In his hurry to set things right in Petz, had Rudi left his own village exposed to even worse trouble?

He refused to think such awful thoughts. He had enough awful things to think about already. "Agatha?" he said. "How did you get ahead of us on the beanstalk? I mean, Susanna and I were there when the beanstalk sprouted. But when we got to Petz, you were already there. How did you manage that?"

Agatha only shook her head. "*I* was there when the beanstalk sprouted, and I didn't see *you*."

Rudi frowned at this. He wanted to believe her. It was possible, wasn't it? Perhaps Agatha had been nearby on the Berg when they had planted the single bean. The ground had shaken so much when the vine had sprouted that perhaps they hadn't even noticed her. "Did you see the Brixen Witch?"

A shrug. "She didn't say she was a witch. She didn't *look* like a witch. At least not any witch that I've ever seen."

"How many witches have you seen?" asked Susanna, awestruck. "Besides your giant *hexenmeister*?"

"Only one, I suppose," admitted Agatha. "But just the same, I know she was a witch."

The beanstalk was sloping downward now. They were more than halfway to the border.

"I looked for you . . . ," said Agatha.

"Me?" Rudi's face burned, and for a moment he forgot about doubting her. "I mean, us? When?"

"After we first met, at the marketplace. Susanna insisted I should have a cow for the beans. Do you remember, Susanna? After we parted, I started thinking that perhaps you weren't joking."

"I wasn't joking," said Susanna Louisa. "I don't know how to tell a joke."

Agatha gave a half smile. "So I tried to find you. To explain that I could not lead a cow through the mountains. But you were already gone."

Rudi halted his downward steps. "*We* tried to find *you!*"

"So that's how we missed one another?" said

Agatha, coming to a stop just behind him. "Each one looking, and neither one standing still long enough to be found?"

"Something like that," muttered Rudi, shifting Hildy in her sack.

Agatha took the Hildy-sack from Rudi and settled it onto her own shoulder. "When I couldn't find you, I walked to Brixen, to explain about the cow."

Rudi stared at her. "You came to Brixen?"

Agatha nodded. "You told me you lived at the dairy, yes? But by the time I found it, the house was dark, and the windows shuttered. So I slept in the barn. I hope you don't mind. *I* didn't mind. It was quite cozy and warm, with the cow and the calf, and the snoring dairyman, and the sweet cat—"

"Wait!" said Rudi. It all sounded like home, and yet . . . it didn't. "What did the cat look like?"

Agatha tilted her head, thinking. "A big cat. Gray and white stripes. Very sweet. Kept me warm all night."

Susanna Louisa gasped. "That's her, Rudi! That's Zick-Zack!"

"Her name is Zick-Zack?" said Agatha, and then she frowned. "What's wrong? She doesn't have fleas, does she?" Agatha hurried to scratch her head.

"The fleas wouldn't dare," said Rudi absently. He continued walking down the slope.

"It's just that Zick-Zack isn't sweet to anyone,"

offered Susanna Louisa, munching on bean pods as she walked. "She's the meanest cat in the whole wide world."

"Ha!" said Agatha. "I told you I have a way with cats. Perhaps I should check my pockets for fish after all."

Susanna laughed at this, but Rudi could not see the humor in this conversation. Something was going on. Agatha wasn't lying now; there could be no mistaking her description of Zick-Zack. And yet, something was wrong.

The beanstalk had become a ladder again, and now they were climbing down. In a matter of minutes they would arrive at the border, near the Brixen Witch's own front door. The witch would have answers for all the questions that filled Rudi's head. At least, he hoped she would.

Agatha continued. "In the morning I went to the house looking for you, but you had already gone. On an errand, the witch said. She pointed the way. And then, before my eyes, the beanstalk grew. That's how I know the old woman was a witch."

And Rudi nearly understood, but not quite. All the pieces of the puzzle were there, but they were laid out wrong. He struggled to rearrange the pieces in his mind.

"The witch," he said. "You met her *after* you climbed the Berg?"

"No, silly," said Agatha. "She answered your door!"

And then some pieces of the puzzle fell into place.

"Agatha! The old woman you met was not a witch. She's my grandmother. And that means the beanstalk you climbed was not—"

"We're here!" announced Agatha. Her feet touched solid ground, and then Susanna's did, and then Rudi's. From inside the burlap sack, Hildy gave a feeble squawk.

They stepped out of the beanstalk's open doorway and found themselves in a familiar place.

"My bean!" cried Susanna. "It sprouted!"

17

Susanna Louisa was right. They were home in Brixen, on the riverbank.

"I knew my bean would sprout! I knew it!"

Rudi stared at Agatha, astounded. "How did you do it?"

"Me?" said Agatha. "I didn't do anything. It must have been the witch. I mean, your grandmother."

There was that unpleasant, nagging feeling again. The feeling that Agatha was not telling him the whole truth. "Oma couldn't have," he told her. "She's not a—"

"Look, Rudi!" said Susanna, pointing. "It's Mama and Papa!" She waved excitedly at her parents, who were standing nearby, gaping at their daughter.

And they were not alone. It looked to Rudi as though half the population of Brixen was milling about on the riverbank and on the footbridge, staring at the beanstalk and murmuring among themselves. A large area around the beanstalk had been roped off to keep the crush of villagers away. Rudi spied Oma standing just beyond the rope, next to a small man with a bald head and a huge mustache. The mayor.

"What are you doing?" said a familiar gruff voice. It was Marco the blacksmith, emerging from behind the beanstalk with a great axe resting on his shoulder. If he'd noticed the three children stepping out from the tangle of vines, he made no sign.

"Master Smith!" Rudi said. "What's going on?"

"No one's allowed inside these here ropes without the mayor's permission," said Marco. "You'd best stay back, and your friends too, until it's your turn."

"Our turn?" said Rudi. "For what?"

"Ah, right. You've been away on an errand, haven't you?" said Marco. He pointed with his thumb at the beanstalk. "So you've missed all the excitement!"

It occurred to Rudi that he hadn't missed *all* the excitement, but he held his tongue. He hoped Susanna Louisa would do the same.

But she wasn't interested in talking just now. She ducked under the rope, ran through the crowd, and leaped into her father's outstretched arms. Her mother shifted a red-faced infant in her arms and bent to cover Susanna with kisses.

"At least the tanner's girl is home safe-like," said Marco. "The way her mother's been carrying on, you'd think the two of you had gone off to the moon, or to Petz, or some such outlandish place."

Rudi gave a weak smile. "We were gone a bit longer than we'd planned."

"And then there's that squalling baby," Marco added, covering an ear with his free hand. "We've had not a moment's peace on our end of the village."

"Master Smith? What are you doing, exactly?"

"Guarding," replied Marco, standing at attention. "On the mayor's orders, on account of this here overgrown weed is causing no end of trouble, but not one of these fools will leave it alone without a bit of convincing. Who's your new friend, anyway?" His face split into a wide grin, and he gave Rudi a jovial nudge. "Did you pluck her from one of them vines?"

Rudi felt hot and itchy. He pulled off his coat and unbuttoned his collar.

Agatha stepped forward and hitched a quick curtsy. "I'm Rudi's cousin. From Klausen."

Marco tipped his cap. "If you say so."

Rudi hurried to change the subject. "You were saying something about trouble. What sort of trouble?"

"First off, there's not a baby in the village won't stop wailing." Marco waved an arm. "The hens won't lay. Your papa's cows won't give milk. It's as if all the simple and innocent creatures is spooked by this monstrous thing. Except *them*." He cocked his head, and now Rudi noticed half a dozen cats sitting around the roped-off circle, intently watching the proceedings.

Rudi's mouth had gone dry. "When did all this start?"

Marco screwed up his face, thinking. "The vine sprouted just after you left on your errand, come to think of it. Some folk say all the strange happenings commenced with the sprouting of the bean plant. Others say it was before." He eyed Rudi and Agatha. "And now here you are, sneaking under the rope to scramble onto the vine, which—I've already told you—is strictly forbidden."

Before Rudi could answer, Agatha tugged at his elbow. "Your grandmother wants a word with you, Rudi. Pleased to meet you, Master Smith." And she pulled Rudi toward Oma, who waited just beyond the rope with her arms folded.

Marco called after them. "If he's your cousin, isn't she *your* grandmother too?" He adjusted the axe on his shoulder and commenced marching around the beanstalk.

Oma bent stiffly to pass beneath the rope, and pulled Rudi a safe distance away from listening ears. "What is that Petz girl doing here again?" She cast a mistrustful eye at Agatha, who was stroking one of the cats.

Rudi's eyebrows shot up, but he kept his voice low. "You know she's from Petz?"

"It's the only place I know where folk dress like that. I knew she was trouble the moment you came home from the Klausen market, babbling about a foreign girl dressed all in shearling."

Rudi recalled that moment. Had it been only yesterday?

Oma tapped him on the head with a knobby finger. "I suppose them keyhole beans came from Petz too. I suppose the Brixen Witch sent you to return them. And," she said, gesturing toward the beanstalk, "I suppose this infernal vegetation has something to do with that too."

Rudi stared at Oma.

She patted his cheek. "Close your mouth, child. I know a thing or two about this and that." Now she tugged him another step farther from the jostling crowd. "Speaking of which, there's more to that shearling girl than meets the eye."

"I know," said Rudi, surprised by his own words.

Oma raised an eyebrow. "She came to the dairy, just as you said she would. She asked for you, but you had already left to visit the old woman. I led her in the direction you'd gone. No sooner had we reached this very spot than the bean sprouted." Oma leaned closer. "Erupted, more like. It was as if the girl had cast a spell on it. It made a monstrous rumbling. Everyone came running. Up she went, and it was all I could do to keep anyone else from doing the same. Can you imagine one of these poor fools climbing that thing and finding himself who-knows-where?"

"In Petz," said Rudi weakly.

Oma gestured toward Marco, who was still marching in a circle. "It's been guarded 'round the clock, but even so, folk keep coming to gape at it. To pluck the beans. Can't say as I blame them, hungry as they are. So the mayor is rationing the beans. Folk are taking turns to harvest what's grown fresh."

"Is Marco right about the trouble?" Rudi asked. "Babies crying and hens not laying?"

Oma nodded. "It's the remaining bit of Petz magic. One magic bean was thrown onto the riverbank. One magic bean is still here somewhere."

Rudi's mouth dropped open again, but then he remembered. "Because there's only so much magic in the world," he said, almost to himself. "That's what the Brixen Witch told us."

"Quite right," said Oma, who knew a thing or two about this and that. She looked up, shading her eyes. "One pod, somewhere on this beanstalk, holds a single keyhole bean. Find it, so your shearling girl can take it back to Petz, and Brixen can be rid of this foreign magic once and for all." Behind them, a cat mewed.

Rudi felt his face burning. "She's not *my* shearling

girl." He craned his neck in an effort to see where the vine led, but it was lost in a cloud. "How will we ever find one keyhole bean? What if it's up there?" Then he gasped. "What if somebody eats it?"

"You'd best hope that doesn't happen." Oma brushed her hands together. "Besides, the mayor has it all in hand. He's offered a reward to anyone who finds a bean with a special mark. A silver florin from the town coffers. And a pint of cream every day for a year, from your papa's cows."

"A pint of cream?" Rudi squinted at her. "That was the mayor's idea?"

She shrugged. "He's a brilliant fellow. For a prize such as that, folk have been quite happy to inspect their beans as they're shelling them. But no keyhole mark as yet."

"Rudi!" A small boy stood at the rope with a basket in hand, hopping and waving.

Rudi waved back. "Hullo, Roger. What are you doing?"

"It's our turn to harvest beans. Isn't that right, mistress? May I start now?"

Oma nodded her permission, and Roger darted under the rope. With a huge gap-toothed grin, he strode past Rudi and began picking.

"Mind the rules," warned Marco. "No eating any beans until they're inspected."

Roger nodded without looking up from his task.

"Oma," said Rudi in a harsh whisper, "the Giant—the witch of Petz—he chased us out of his fortress. I don't think he followed us down the vine, but might he still?"

Oma frowned. "Did you return the pouch of beans?"

"Yes!" Rudi hissed. "Agatha put them back in the Giant's storehouse, where she'd found them."

Oma cast one more glance at Agatha, who stood at a polite distance while several cats wound themselves around her ankles. "I don't know why he would chase you, then."

From behind him, Rudi heard a muffled *cluck*. The blood drained from his head. He retrieved the burlap sack and held it out to her.

"Maybe it's because we took this."

18

Oma pulled open the sack. With a flurry of feathers, Hildy popped out and fluttered to the ground. Then, as if nothing at all unusual had happened, she began to scratch and peck at the grass.

Oma stared at Rudi in disbelief. "Why in the name of all that's magic did you steal a chicken from the witch of Petz?"

Rudi shrugged weakly. "Susanna wouldn't leave without her. I didn't know what else to do."

"Where is that tanner's girl?" said Oma through gritted teeth. "I need to have a word with her."

Rudi scanned the crowd for Susanna Louisa, and finally spied her playing in the near meadow. He called to her, and she came bouncing over.

"Did you see, mistress? Rudi saved Hildy from that

nasty mean *hexenmeister*!" She scooped up the hen and stroked her feathers.

"Shhh!" hissed Oma. "There will be no talk of such things. That hen needs to go back where she came from." She lifted Hildy out of Susanna's arms and turned around. "You, child! Shearling girl, come here."

Agatha extracted herself from the mewling cats and came to stand before Oma. Their eyes locked in mutual respect and wariness. "Good day, mistress," said Agatha with a curtsy.

"Here you are again, child," said Oma. "I thought we were well rid of you—nothing personal. But since you're here, you can do us a favor. As soon as the missing keyhole bean is found, you may deliver it, along with this here chicken, to its rightful owner." She dropped the hen into Agatha's arms. "I presume you know who that is."

"But, mistress!" wailed Susanna. "Agatha can't take Hildy back to Petz. I'm her rightful owner! I can prove it." She turned to Agatha, who, as instructed, tilted Hildy into a legs-up position. The little hen kicked in protest. Rudi gently grasped her scaly feet and held them as still as he could. Oma tapped her foot in exasperation.

Susanna Louisa peered at Hildy's fat legs. "She has a scar here . . . on her leg . . . somewhere . . ." She brushed the fluffy feathers with a finger, separating them gently. "Here!" she declared triumphantly. Then her brow furrowed. "What's this?" Her face paled. "Oops." She looked to Rudi, who forced himself to peer more closely at the hen's underside.

He gulped. "Not a scar," he said, showing Oma. "A keyhole mark."

They all looked at Susanna Louisa. Susanna looked at the hen in Agatha's arms, who was now turned upright.

"Hildy?" Susanna reached to stroke her plump breast. The hen pecked at her.

Susanna jumped back, startled and dismayed. "This is not my hen! Hildy would never peck me!" Her face grew red, and tears welled in her eyes. Despite all the trouble she had caused, Rudi's heart melted for her. "My mama needs me," Susanna said in a small voice, and she darted away.

For a moment they all stared after her. The hen who was not Hildy clucked indignantly in Agatha's arms.

Before anyone could say another word, Roger came running over and elbowed his way into their midst.

"I found something! See what I found?" In his hand lay a bean pod, split open to reveal a row of smooth, white beans. One of the beans bore a black mark in the unmistakable shape of a keyhole.

"Is this a special bean?" said Roger. "It has a mark on it. See?"

Fast as a whip, Oma swiped at Roger's open palm. But Not-Hildy was faster, because Not-Hildy was hungry. Her head shot forward in a speckled blur, and she cleanly pecked a single bean from the pod in Roger's hand. Then she settled herself again in Agatha's arms, shook out her tail feathers, and swallowed.

They stared at the hen in surprise. Now Roger held an open pod with a row of unblemished white beans, and an empty space where one bean used to be.

"She ate the special bean!" cried Roger, his face turning red. He scowled at Agatha. "Give it back!"

"I didn't take it," said Agatha. "The chicken did!"

"Tell her to spit it out! That's my bean! I found it!"

Oma stepped between them. "Quite right, lad, yes, we all saw it, good lad, you've won the prize! Master Mayor, give this fine young lad his reward and send him along home, that's a good lad." She patted Roger on the head and waved the mayor over.

The mayor ducked under the rope and addressed the milling crowd. "The special bean has been found. The reward is claimed!" He made a show of shaking Roger's hand and presenting him with a shiny silver florin. Roger's fury gave way to a broad smile. The villagers half-cheered and half-grumbled. There was scattered applause.

"That makes things easier to carry," said Oma cheerfully. She spun Agatha by the shoulders and prodded her toward the beanstalk. "Best of luck to you then, Godspeed and all that, my thanks for bringing my grandson back in one piece, now up you go."

"No!" said Agatha, clutching the hen tightly to her chest. "Begging your pardon, mistress, but we made a bargain, Rudi and I."

Oma glared at her, but Agatha held Oma's gaze and lifted her chin.

"She's right." Rudi stepped alongside Agatha. "She helped us return the beans. We couldn't have done it without her. And so I promised to take her—" He struggled to find the right words. It was bad luck to talk of such things. But what if you *needed* to talk of such things? "We need to climb the Berg so she can ask for advice."

"There's no time for that!" Oma said, jabbing Rudi's shoulder with a finger. "What if the Petz witch comes down this vine after all? Enchanted beans are one thing. Even enchanted chickens. But now an enchanted chicken has eaten an enchanted bean. That's magic upon magic, and that sounds like trouble to me. If you want to go home, girl, you need to go now, because this beanstalk must come down, and the sooner the better. Before that witch from Petz gets tired of waiting for his treasure."

Rudi's mind scrambled for a response. He did not want to disobey Oma. Besides, she was probably right, as usual. They could not put the entire village in danger because of a hungry chicken.

But Agatha needed Rudi's help too. And he had promised her.

"Oma," he tried again. "There is another way back to Petz. Another beanstalk, up on the Berg. We can visit the . . . old woman . . . and then Agatha can go home that way. We can cut this beanstalk down, and Brixen will be safe." He drew in a breath and said once more, "We made a bargain."

"You shouldn't make a bargain you can't keep," Oma snapped. Then she sighed and shook her head. "But I suppose it's too late for that." She waggled a finger at Agatha. "I hope never to lay eyes on you or that chicken again. Nothing personal."

From the safety of Agatha's arms, Not-Hildy gave an apologetic squawk. She kept a beady eye on the collection of cats that had once again come to wind themselves around Agatha's ankles.

Oma called once more for the mayor, who hurried over and conferred with her in whispers and animated gestures. She pointed toward the beanstalk. He shook his head in vigorous disagreement. She plopped her hands on her hips and tapped her foot. He wiped his bald head with a handkerchief. He sighed. He bowed his head. He turned to face the crowd, which was still murmuring and gossiping and milling as if it were a holiday.

"Attention, everyone!" announced the mayor. He waited for the crowd to settle into a restless silence. "It has come to my attention that this beanstalk is, er, unsafe." He glanced toward Oma, who gave an encouraging nod. "It must be cut down before it falls down."

"But what about the beans?" someone called from the crowd. "After the awful winter we had?"

"That's right," said another voice. "You wouldn't take the supper from my children's mouths, would you?" A ripple of agreement rolled through the crowd.

The mayor pulled at his collar and cleared his throat. "Certainly not," he said. "But we can't have this vine come crashing down on anyone unawares. It's your children's safety I'm thinking of."

The crowd gave a collective grumble.

The mayor glanced once more at Oma, who eyed the crowd with a scowl. She chewed the inside of her cheek. Then she stepped forward and whispered something into the mayor's ear.

He raised his hands to quiet the villagers. "Once the beanstalk is down, you will have your fill of beans." He waved toward the gigantic vine. "There are beans uncountable on this plant! I suggest you all go home and gather your baskets and buckets. But stay safe inside your cottages until the task is done. I don't want anyone in harm's way when this monstrous thing comes down."

With that, the mayor turned his back on the crowd, and the announcement was finished. The villagers stood for a moment, letting his words settle into their brains. Then they burst into action. They scrambled and scurried in every direction, flowing away from the riverbank and toward their cottages to do what the mayor had advised.

"Well done, Your Honor," Oma told the mayor. She turned to Marco, who stood at attention with his axe on his shoulder. "Ready, Master Smith?"

Marco thrust out his chest. "Yes, mistress. With pleasure."

Just then came a loud squawk from the hen in Agatha's arms. Not-Hildy fluttered furiously and flapped to the ground. She ran in tight circles and then settled onto the grass, clucking quietly to herself. The cats at Agatha's feet watched her, as if they'd never seen such a bold chicken.

"What's wrong?" said Agatha. "I didn't hurt her, did I?"

"There's nothing wrong," said Oma. "She's getting ready to lay."

Marco pushed his cap back on his head and laughed. "Well, how do you like that? Just the mention of cutting down this here vine is enough to set things straight. Why didn't we think of that before?"

In rapt silence they all watched Not-Hildy. Rudi understood what Marco was saying. If the hen could lay an egg, it meant the enchantment must be over, or nearly so. In any case, it would be a hopeful sign.

Not-Hildy sat as still as a stone, as if she were thinking about something very important. The cats twitched their tails, but kept a wary distance. A single gray cloud drifted across the face of the sun.

Suddenly Not-Hildy fluttered her wings and stood up. With a satisfied squawk, she shook herself out and commenced pecking in the grass for seeds and bugs.

Rudi stepped to the spot where Not-Hildy had been sitting. He carefully brushed at the long grass until he found what he was looking for. His eyes grew wide, and he sat back on his heels, staring. In the distance, thunder rumbled.

"Oma?" he said. "What color should a hen's egg be?"

"What kind of silly question is that? White or brown, most always. Why? What color egg does a speckled hen from Petz lay?"

Rudi lifted the egg to show her. "Golden."

19

"**Let me see** that egg," said Oma, holding out her hand.

In the sky above, rainclouds gathered, blotting the sun. Thunder rolled. The collection of cats hissed at the impending rain, and scampered away to their secret corners.

Rudi handed over the egg carefully, though somehow he was sure it would not break. It was very heavy, for an egg.

"What's *that*?" came a small voice from behind Rudi.

"Roger! What are you doing here?" A fat raindrop hit Rudi's head.

"I forgot my bean basket," Roger said, staring at

the egg in Oma's hand. She quickly dropped it into her apron pocket. But it was too heavy, and it tore through the threadbare fabric and fell onto the grass.

"You should be at home!" she said, covering the egg with her foot. "Indoors, safe-like. Didn't you hear the mayor? This beanstalk is coming down."

Roger didn't move. His stunned gaze shifted from Oma's foot to the axe on Marco's shoulder. Its handle was as long as Roger was tall.

The sky grew darker. Thunder rumbled again, closer now. Rain began to fall.

Rudi scanned the ground near the beanstalk. Spying Roger's basket, he plucked it from the grass and handed it to him. "Best be going now," he said.

Still staring, Roger nodded slowly and backed away. Then he ducked under the barrier rope and dashed toward home, scattering bean pods in his wake. Rudi heard his voice over the rising wind. "Konrad! Wait'll I tell you what I just saw!"

Oma motioned for Rudi to retrieve the egg from the grass and hand it to her. "Master Smith? Time's wasting, and I'm getting wet." She wiggled her fingers through the hole in her pocket. "My best apron," she muttered.

Marco weighed his axe and circled the beanstalk, taking its measure.

Blinking the raindrops from his eyes, Rudi hurried

to pull Oma outside the rope barrier and up the slope of the riverbank. Agatha scooped up Not-Hildy and followed them as thunder rolled across the sky.

Finally Marco was ready. He spat on his palms, rubbed them together, and hefted the axe, adjusting his grip on the thick wooden handle.

Rudi held his breath.

In one powerful motion Marco lifted the great axe from his shoulder and swung it through the air.

At that same moment there came a blast of thunder that shook the ground.

FUM!

Rudi and Agatha exchanged a horrified look.

WHACK. The axe head struck the beanstalk and sliced through a vine as thick as Rudi's arm.

FUM!

"Oma," croaked Rudi, "that is not ordinary thunder."

"I didn't think so," said Oma, her gaze fixed on Marco. "Master Smith," she said calmly. "Keep going."

Marco swung the axe again, and again, working his way around the huge tangle of vines. *WHACK. WHACK. WHACK.*

FUMM!

"He's coming!" Agatha hissed in a desperate whisper.

Marco's brow furrowed upon hearing these words, but he did not look up from his task. With a sleeve he wiped sweat and rain from his face, and he swung the axe again.

WHACK.

The beanstalk began to buckle.

FUMM!

WHACK.

Then, from high overhead, Rudi heard a crackling and a rustling. It grew louder and closer, gathering itself into a rush, and then a roar, as the beanstalk came crashing toward the ground.

Rudi shut his eyes and covered his head. Beside him, Oma gasped. Agatha stifled a scream. Not-Hildy squawked. A blast of wind hit Rudi as the beanstalk fell, knocking him off his feet. The ground shook as if the sky itself were falling.

Then all was still. The rain stopped. The wind died away. Not a single bird dared to sing. Even the river itself seemed hushed.

Away in the distance, thunder rumbled and faded away.

Rudi opened one eye, and then the other.

Before him lay the beanstalk. It had fallen across the river, narrowly missing the footbridge, and created another bridge, of sorts. It snaked away across the near meadow and toward the Berg, its upper end disappearing in the pine forest that carpeted the lower slopes of the mountain. On the riverbank a ragged green stump remained, hacked and torn. Bean pods and leaves littered the ground. The stakes supporting the rope barrier had been ripped from the ground by the force of the fall.

Rudi scrambled to his feet and helped Oma up. "Are you all right?"

"Fine, fine," she answered, brushing leaves from her skirts, the golden egg still in her hand. "Right as rain. Well done, Master Smith." Then she frowned. "Master Smith?"

Rudi's stomach knotted. "Marco?" He took a step toward the fallen beanstalk. "Where is he?"

"Under here!" came a voice from somewhere near the footbridge.

Rudi and Agatha scrambled down the riverbank in the direction of the voice. After a few frantic moments Marco popped out of the water, clinging to the fallen beanstalk.

"Lucky thing I fell into the river," he said, water running in rivulets down his face. "That beanstalk would've crushed me if I'd been on solid ground." He pulled himself along the vine toward the riverbank, where Rudi offered a hand to hoist him up. "Is everyone all right up here?"

They all nodded. Not-Hildy squawked in Agatha's arms.

"He's gone," declared Agatha, scanning the horizon in all directions. "Brixen is saved!"

Rudi heaved a sigh of relief.

Oma tilted her head, listening. "Let's hope so. I don't trust that foreign witch."

"How's that, mistress?" said Marco, wiggling a finger in his ear. "Did I hear you mention a—"

Oma waved a hand. "Your ears is waterlogged, Master Smith. I can't tell you how grateful we are. You've saved the village from that hazard."

"Two hazards, or so it seems," muttered Marco, winking at Rudi. "Glad to do it, mistress." And he tipped his dripping cap to Oma, who nodded in reply.

Rudi offered his hand stiffly. "Thank you," he told Marco, and he meant it, yet somehow it bothered him to say it.

"Ah," said Marco, looking past Rudi. "Here they come."

And so they were. The villagers of Brixen had emerged from their cottages and workshops, and now they streamed toward the riverbank and the fallen beanstalk with their baskets, sacks, and pails.

The mayor was one of the first to arrive. He took a position on the footbridge, raised his arms, and cleared his throat.

"It seems fitting to say a few words on this noteworthy occasion," he said, to scattered groans and coughs.

"Master Smith here single-handedly disposed of the gigantic mysterious beanstalk, which had become a danger and a hazard, despite also being very delicious."

There was a smattering of applause.

The mayor beckoned to Marco to join him on the bridge. "On behalf of the entire village, I thank you. We are forever in your debt, for you are a true hero of Brixen." As the crowd applauded, the mayor shook Marco's hand, then grabbed his soggy shoulders and kissed him on both cheeks. Marco blushed. The crowd cheered.

"And now," announced the mayor, "it's harvest time!"

The crowd cheered again. They scampered across the footbridge, settled along the fallen vine, and began harvesting the beans from the fallen beanstalk that had once extended all the way to Petz.

Rudi felt a nudge at his elbow.

"So," said Oma. "What do you think of our new hero?"

"Happy for him," said Rudi immediately. "Very happy, good for him. I've always liked Marco, good for him."

"You're babbling," Oma said.

Rudi's face burned.

"Don't worry." She patted his shoulder. "Your time will come. Though, when it does, you may wish you were still a bystander."

20

By nightfall the news had spread through the entire village. Not even the biggest crop of beans after the leanest winter in memory was enough to distract the townsfolk of Brixen when an interesting rumor surfaced.

It had started with Roger. He'd told his brother Konrad, and had been overheard by their friend Nicolas, who'd found Rudi, who had escaped to the milking barn in search of solitude.

"The foreign girl has a hen that lays golden eggs!" said Nicolas, breathless. "Konrad said that Roger said you saw her lay one. Did you?"

Rudi had known this was coming, but it vexed him anyway. And it had happened more quickly than he'd expected. "Did I see the foreign girl lay a golden egg? No."

He carried the milking stool to Rosie's stall.

"Very funny, Rudi."

Rudi settled on the stool and rubbed Rosie's flank. "Who else did Roger tell?"

"Nobody," said Nicolas. "Only Konrad, but he's Roger's big brother, so Roger had to tell him. That's all."

Rudi squinted at him and waited.

"Well . . . ," said Nicolas. "Of course they told their mama, but what can you do when your mother asks you a question? And mothers and fathers aren't allowed to keep secrets from each other, so I expect their papa knows too. And I think Mistress Tanner and Mistress Gerta might have heard Roger telling his mother. But that's all." Nicolas took a deep breath. "Nobody, really."

There was no point in getting upset. It didn't change anything. Rudi still had one more errand to run. It would be tricky, though, now that news of the golden egg was spreading. People would object to having this newfound wealth taken from them. Rudi guessed that Oma would tell him to climb the Berg at first light, so that he and Agatha might escape the attention of curious neighbors asking where they thought they were going with that there chicken.

"I'm busy," Rudi said to Nicolas without looking up. "But—"

"I don't know where it is." He knew what Nicolas

wanted to ask. "My Oma put it away. Someplace safe."

Nicolas's shoulders slumped. "I wouldn't have told anyone." He turned and left the barn.

As he tended to Rosie, Rudi breathed deeply. The cows could always tell if he was upset or worried, and it worried them, too. And poor Rosie was already spooked. Just as Marco had reported, she'd given barely a drop of milk all day. Even now her udder was soft, not full and swollen with milk as it ought to be. Nearby, her newborn calf watched patiently. If the calf didn't have a meal soon, she would starve, and that would be more than Rudi or his family could bear.

All because of the foreign magic.

Rudi knew it was up to him and Agatha to take the Giant's treasure back where it belonged. And it would be even more treacherous this time, because this time the Giant would be waiting for them.

He wished he could set out before daybreak. But it would be folly to venture up the Berg in the dark.

And what if Rudi failed in his task? He could hardly bear to think of what might happen then. Why was such a huge task left to him, anyway? He was only thirteen years old. Why couldn't someone else do it? Marco was strong and brave. He was a true hero. The mayor had said so. Marco was the perfect person for the job.

Rosie gave a long, low *Mooooo*.

"Sorry, Rosie," said Rudi. He gently rubbed her

bristly coat. "It seems neither one of us is in the mood."
On his way out of the barn, Rudi caught a glimpse of
Zick-Zack. She arched her back and hissed at him, then
darted away into the shadows.

Inside the house, the mood was no better. Oma
rocked in her chair as if to keep the rug from flying
away. Mama fluttered around the kitchen, trying to pre-
pare a meal of mostly beans. Out the back window Rudi
saw Agatha tending Not-Hildy, who was quarantined in
a little pen of her own, away from the view of inquisitive
neighbors.

Papa shook his head at the collection of baskets
piled high with beans. "Plenty of food at last, but what
good will it do if the cows won't milk?" he said. "Oma,
are you sure we can't sell that egg at market? Think of
what it could buy. We're on the brink of disaster here."

"Sit down to dinner, and don't ask me such a
thing." Oma scowled and rocked. "Unless you want a
true disaster on our hands." She motioned Rudi closer.
"Tomorrow morning, at first light," she whispered.

And there it was. Rudi wished he could refuse to go.
But there was no refusing Oma.

What would the Brixen Witch think, seeing him in
trouble yet again? She'd probably think that he was the
wrong person to be dealing with such things.

More and more, Rudi thought she might be right.

There came a knock at the door.

It was the mayor, red in the face and twitchy in the fingers. He nodded a greeting to Mama and Papa. But when he noticed Rudi, he removed his hat and bowed hastily. "Good day, Master Rudi," he said.

Rudi felt the color rise in his face.

"Now what?" said Oma, not bothering with niceties.

The mayor rotated his hat in his hands. "Well, mistress, there seems to be a bit of scuttlebutt regarding that remarkable hen of yours." His gaze darted around the room.

"What are you looking for?" Oma snapped. "Do you think we're the type of folk who keep chickens in the house?"

"Certainly not!" the mayor said. His hat rotated more quickly. "At any rate, I've had a number of inquiries about that chicken. It seems the good folk of Brixen want to know what's to become of the remarkable egg that your remarkable chicken laid on the riverbank this afternoon."

Oma stared at him. Her rocking chair creaked. The mayor squirmed. Oma looked pleased.

The mayor tried again. "You see, mistress, it was a difficult winter, if you'll recall."

Oma continued staring and rocking.

"And the townsfolk, you see, are wondering about this newfound bounty, which quite clearly came about because of the mysterious gigantic beanstalk . . . which, seeing as it was so large, was more or less everyone's business. . . ."

"Yes, yes," said Oma, running short on patience. "Everyone has had their share of beans, have they not?"

"Oh, yes, mistress," the mayor hurried to say. "Everyone is enjoying them so much that they're already getting sick of them!" He cleared his throat. "So you see, it's not the beans, really. It's the other thing. From the hen?" He scanned the room once more.

"What about it?"

The mayor took a deep breath. "Some folk are saying the egg should be sold, and the proceeds divided up amongst the whole village."

Oma rocked in her chair so hard, it inched across the room. The mayor took a stuttering step backward.

"Now you listen to me, Master Mayor. That hen is not mine, and neither is her egg. And no one else in Brixen can make any claim to them neither. They're going back where they belong. You think that beanstalk was trouble? Believe me, you don't want to see what kind of trouble that egg can cause."

The mayor nodded nervously. The hat turned. "What shall I tell folk, then?"

"Tell them whatever you like. Tell them I fried the egg and ate it for dinner."

The mayor raised his eyebrows. "Yes. Well. I'll think of something to tell them. All my best to you,

Master Rudi." He bowed once more, plopped his hat onto his head, and left the house.

Oma rocked forward, grabbed the door, and slammed it shut after him. She muttered to herself, thinking. Then she looked up, surprised. "What are you looking at?"

Rudi cleared his throat. "Where is it, anyway?"

With a sly grin, Oma reached into her mended apron pocket, drew out the golden egg, and held it up for everyone to see. "They can say all they like about it, but it won't matter a bit. At first light tomorrow it's going back where it belongs. Isn't that so, Rudi?"

Rudi nodded miserably. Mama gave a worried *tsk*. Papa blew his nose.

There came another knock at the door.

"Now what?"

Rudi opened it. "Oh, hullo, Roger."

Roger held out an empty cream pitcher. "I'm here for my reward."

Rudi scratched the back of his head. "Sorry. But it seems our cows aren't milking at the moment. We'll have to owe you."

"Oh," said Roger, but his disappointment didn't last long. "Can you come out and play?"

Before Rudi could answer, they heard a loud squawk through the back window. Then a voice: "Oh dear!"

"Agatha?" said Mama. "What's wrong, child?"

"Nothing's wrong, exactly," said Agatha, appearing in the window. "It's just . . . this." She held up another golden egg.

"Put that away!" cried Oma, but it was too late.

Roger's eyes grew wide. The empty cream pitcher dropped to the floor with a crash, and he dashed out the door.

"Konrad! Wait'll I tell you what I just saw!"

21

Rudi could not sleep. For the second time in as many days, he lay awake in his bed, waiting for morning and thinking about the errand he did not want to run. His knapsack lay just inside the front door, the two precious eggs wrapped and hidden deep within.

The villagers had heard about the second golden egg. They had visited the Bauer farm in a steady stream all evening, trying in turns to cajole Oma, or argue, or threaten her, into handing over the eggs. But Oma would have none of it. She cajoled and argued and threatened right back.

Still, they tried. The mayor argued that things had changed in the short time since his first visit. It was no small feat for a hen to lay two eggs in one day, not to mention two such remarkable eggs. With a little luck, every family in Brixen might have their own egg before long. What could it hurt to wait, and return Not-Hildy to her owner in a week or so? "We needn't tell him what his hen's been doing," the mayor added with a knowing wink. "He'll never be the wiser."

Mistress Tanner nearly pushed her squalling baby through the open window, demanding to know how Oma could be so selfish as to keep those eggs for herself, without regard for a helpless babe who could not speak for itself.

Even Marco the blacksmith, who had witnessed for himself the enchanted nature of the chicken and her eggs (and who, in any case, should have known better than to argue with Oma), declared that if seven-year-old Roger could earn a silver florin just for finding a bean, he himself should have at least one golden egg for relieving the village of the mysterious beanstalk. Especially now that Oma had two.

And so it went into the night. Finally, Papa had barred the door and latched the shutters tight, and ordered Rudi to keep his slingshot close at hand against the possibility of a more serious confrontation.

Perhaps, Rudi had thought, Marco was not the perfect person to deal with witchy business after all.

But now, as he lay in the dark, Rudi was convinced that *he* was not the right person either. He thought of the awkward respect his neighbors showed him, just because he'd had dealings with the Brixen Witch. At first it had made him feel important. But did he really want to live his whole life that way? Standing apart from everyone else. Being pointed at. Whispered about. And for what? So people could pester him with selfish requests, and go away muttering, or worse, if he gave them an answer they didn't like? To think he'd been jealous of Marco, even for a moment. Marco could have the attention. He was welcome to it.

Rudi punched his pillow and flopped onto his stomach. Why did anyone need to go with Agatha at all? She'd managed to travel to Klausen by herself in the first place, even crossing the border unharmed. She could certainly carry the magic back to Petz by herself. She even had the other beanstalk to make the going easier. She'd be perfectly all right on her own.

The more Rudi thought about it, the more certain he became that there was nothing he could do. In fact, he would only be in the way.

He rolled onto his back.

It was decided, then. He would tell them in the morning. He would give Agatha the golden eggs, and the chicken, and the warm clothing he'd borrowed from her father, and send her on her way. He might even give her a good-bye kiss. It would be fitting on such an occasion.

But he could not quiet his mind. He tried not to think about the Giant, who must be growing more furious with each golden egg laid by the stolen hen. He tried not to think about Ludwig, and all the decent people of Petz, condemned by their witch to live always on the brink of starvation, in a never-ending winter. He tried not to think that once Agatha walked out his front door, he would most likely never see her again.

From the barn across the yard came the lowing of a cow, and then the bleating of a calf. "Don't worry, little one," Rudi whispered. "Soon the Petz magic will be gone and everything in Brixen will be back to normal. Your mama will give milk again."

The calf bleated once more. She sounded hungry.

Rudi lay in the dark and stared at the rafters, and tried not to tell himself that there could be only one way to know for sure that the foreign magic was safely and completely out of Brixen.

He kicked at his covers.

Why should it be his responsibility, anyway?

He couldn't think of any reason why. He only knew that it *was*.

He would be going to Petz.

Why was the morning so slow in coming?

Finally Rudi gave up trying to sleep. He would double-check the contents of his knapsack, and he would get dressed, so that when first light came, he'd be ready.

He crept down the stairs to find Oma sitting and rocking in the dim light of the fireplace embers.

"Why are you up?" he asked her. He stirred the embers, waking the fire.

Oma's chair creaked. "Couldn't sleep."

Rudi began gathering his things. He dropped a few beans into a burlap sack so that Not-Hildy would have something to eat along the way. He made sure Ludwig's mittens and fur-lined hat were packed safely in his knapsack, and he added warm clothing of his own for the journey home.

"You're a good lad," came Oma's voice from the shadows.

Rudi looked up from his task. Somehow those few words were almost enough to make him feel better. It was as if she knew and understood all his doubts.

He tiptoed to the window and swung the shutters open, so that he would see the first hint of light when it touched the eastern sky. But all was black and quiet. Even the moon had gone to bed.

Rudi pulled on his boots and coat. "I'll go out to wake Agatha."

She had insisted upon sleeping in the barn. She'd said she preferred it to sleeping indoors, which would remind her too much of home and of her father, who must be worried sick about her by now.

Poor Ludwig. Rudi had made a promise to him, too. Going all the way to Petz was the right thing to do, after all. He could see Ludwig once more, and thank him properly for his kindness. He could personally return his hat and his mittens, and his daughter. He could witness Ludwig's joy and relief at seeing Agatha safely home again.

"Keep an eye on that one," said Oma. "She's agreeable enough, and I know she's your friend. Goodness knows it's no picnic living in Petz. But there's something about her I don't trust. There's things she isn't telling us."

Rudi knew what she meant. "Oma? How does an enchanted beanstalk grow from a magic bean, anyway?"

"What makes you think I know such things?" Oma rocked, and creaked.

Rudi shrugged. "Agatha says . . . she says you did something at the riverbank to make it sprout." He looked at his grandmother sidelong. "She thinks you're a witch."

"Does she, now? That's funny. Because I say *she* did something to make it sprout."

"How could she? Doesn't it take a witch, or at least someone who knows about magic? You know some things about magic, don't you?"

"So do you. And so does that tanner's girl, from what I've seen, but neither of *you* could make it sprout. How do you explain that?"

Rudi shook his head. He couldn't. And yet something nagged at his mind. What had the Brixen Witch said about the gift for magic? That it was partly a gift of nature and partly something a person could learn, through practice.

But he had more pressing things to think about right now. He buttoned his coat and left the dark house to venture across the dark yard to the dark barn.

He found Agatha already walking toward the house. "Zick-Zack woke me," she said. "Silly cat was purring so loudly. She does that just before she goes off to catch her breakfast. I wonder why she woke so early today?"

"She was probably thinking about eating *you* for breakfast," said Rudi, who still didn't trust Zick-Zack.

Agatha gave a half smile. "Perhaps she wanted to say good-bye."

Rudi was tempted to offer Zick-Zack to Agatha as a gift, but he changed his mind. Zick-Zack was not truly his to offer. She belonged to no one but herself.

And besides, Petz had enough troubles without Zick-Zack.

22

Inside the house, Oma paced. "It's springtime. The sun should be coming up earlier every day. Where is it today?"

Rudi had never seen her so anxious. But he knew how she felt.

"I heard the steeple clock chime five times yesterday just before dawn," he said, in an effort to ease her mind. Though, on this night he'd been so distraught that he hadn't heard the clock at all.

Oma shook a nervous finger at him. "Quite right. Good lad. If the sun's not up by the time the clock chimes five, you'll go then anyway."

"Why don't we go now?" said Agatha. "Before anyone else is awake?"

Oma shook her head. "You'd need torches, and that

would attract attention. The night watchman would love a golden egg as much as anybody, and you've seen how no one in this village can keep his mouth shut. No, best to wait until dawn. But not a moment later. The last thing we need is for that infernal hen to see the sunrise and be inspired to lay another golden egg."

Rudi shuddered to think what might happen if Not-Hildy laid a third egg.

They waited for the clock to chime, and paced along with Oma, until Rudi thought they would worry a hole in the rug.

Finally it happened. The steeple clock began to peal.

They sprang into a flurry of activity as Rudi counted the chimes.

One . . .

They threw on their coats.

Two . . .

Agatha shook out the burlap sack and opened the back door.

Three . . .

Rudi stuffed a sleepy Not-Hildy into the sack and gently tied it shut.

Four . . .

Oma kissed each of them for luck and pushed them out the door into the predawn blackness.

Five . . .

Rudi heaved a sigh of relief. They were on their way.

Before this day was out, their ordeal would be over.

Six . . .

They looked at each other in disbelief. "How did we—"

Seven . . .

Rudi shook himself. The eastern sky was as black as the sky above his head. Something was wrong. Very wrong.

Eight.

Rudi and Agatha stood rooted in place, too horrified to move or to think.

The chiming stopped.

Eight o'clock.

"What's going on?" squeaked Agatha. "Someone is in the clock tower playing a trick, yes?"

Rudi wished she were right, but he knew it could not be so. The steeple clock was sacred ground, in more ways than one. It was the only timepiece in Brixen. No one could afford a clock of their own, but no one really needed one. They had other ways to tell the time. Roosters crowed; dogs and chickens asked to be fed; cows demanded to be milked. And, of course, like clockwork, the sun moved across the sky.

Until today.

"It's not a trick," said Rudi. "I fear it's the trouble our witch told us about. It means the Giant has finally broken the rules."

"Rules?" said Agatha. "What rules?"

"Rules for witches," came another voice in the darkness. "One witch at a time."

Rudi couldn't see who it was, but he didn't need to. He knew that voice.

"Susanna Louisa! What are you doing here?"

"I heard about the second golden egg. I thought you might be leaving this morning, and here you are! I wanted to say good-bye." Her shadowy form pushed a shadowy something at Agatha. "Thank you for letting me borrow these."

"Papa's things." Agatha pocketed Ludwig's shearling mittens. She wrapped the woolen scarf around her neck, though the air was not cold.

"Is that what's happening, Rudi?" said Susanna. "The Giant has crossed the border into Brixen?"

Rudi gulped. He could not bring himself to answer her.

"You can fix it, Rudi," said Susanna, as if she could hear his most secret thoughts. "I know you can. You're the smartest person in the whole village. Besides, the Petz witch has no power in Brixen."

Rudi blinked at her. "What did you say?"

"Remember, Rudi?" said Susanna. "When the Brixen Witch sent us to Petz with the beans? She told us we'd be on our own, because she has no power in Petz."

Rudi thought for a moment. "Yes," he said. "I do remember that."

"Well," said Susanna. "The rules are the same for everyone, right?"

Now Agatha chimed in. "If the Giant has no power in Brixen, how has he kept the sun from coming up?"

"I don't think *he's* the one doing it," said Rudi. "But I think it's happening *because* of what he did. He's upset the balance. Something like that." Rudi wished he were better at understanding witches.

"Come with us, Susanna," said Agatha.

Rudi opened his mouth to protest, but something made him change his mind.

On their journey to Petz and back, Susanna Louisa had caused more trouble than any nine-year-old girl ought to cause. She'd been flighty, and a pest, and a burden. She'd made some drastic errors (Rudi adjusted the Not-Hildy sack on his shoulder), and yet . . .

And yet, she'd been brave when Rudi had faltered. She'd cheered him with her innocent chatter and had made him feel . . . capable. He had been responsible for her, and perhaps that was her most important purpose—to remind Rudi of everything about home that he loved. Susanna Louisa *was* Brixen. Without her, Rudi might never have gotten as far as Petz. And he might never have gotten home again.

Was she clever, as the Brixen Witch had said? Did

she have a natural talent for conferring with such folk as witches—a skill he was still struggling mightily to learn? Or was she simply so trusting, and so full of faith, that it only seemed that way?

"Yes," he said finally. "Come with us. My Oma is watching from our doorway, see? She'll tell your mama that you've gone on another one of our harmless little errands." He attempted a smile and a wink, but it didn't feel very convincing. For the briefest moment he was glad it was still dark.

"Please come," said Agatha. "You can give the scarf and mittens to Papa yourself. He would like that too."

But Susanna Louisa shook her head in the gloom. "I think maybe not this time. I need to feed the hens. Rudi, can you tell the Brixen Witch I'll visit her again sometime?"

Rudi blinked at her, but he nodded. "I will."

"And give her this." She put a small smooth object into Rudi's hand.

"An egg?" he said.

"A real egg. From the real Hildy."

"Aren't you worried it will break?"

"I know you'll keep it safe. Rudi, we never did tell Agatha about the snow finch, did we? I think perhaps you ought to tell her about the snow finch."

"Clever girl," said Rudi, and he meant it. "I will, I promise."

Now the small shadowy figure of Susanna turned to face Agatha. "And give this to your papa too." She threw her arms around Agatha, who hugged her in return.

For one more moment, Rudi was glad it was too dark for anyone to see his face. He carefully wrapped and pocketed Hildy's egg. "We should be going," he said quietly.

"I'll be waiting for you, Rudi," Susanna told him. "I'll see you when you're back from fixing things." And she turned and ran, and disappeared into the darkness.

23

They picked and fumbled their way up the Berg as best they could in the darkness. But Rudi had spent nearly every day of his life on the slopes of this mountain, and so they made quicker progress than he'd expected.

The fallen beanstalk snaked its way across the near meadow, and up to the forest and the high meadow, as if it knew the way. Agatha could have managed on her own after all, Rudi decided. Still, he was glad to be going with her now.

They walked in silence, to avoid the attention of inquisitive villagers or errant witches. Rudi soon became lost in his own thoughts. Would their witch be able to help Agatha win the summer back? Would they even have the chance to ask her? Or would the Brixen

Witch be under siege herself from the marauding witch of Petz?

And then as they climbed, Rudi realized something was different. The change was so gradual, he barely noticed it at first. But after a few minutes, there could be no mistake.

The sun was coming up.

"Has he gone?" said Agatha.

"It seems so," answered Rudi. "At least for now."

Soon they reached the crevice in the mountain. The Brixen Witch's front door.

Rudi knocked.

No answer.

He knocked again, harder.

"I'm not at home," came a familiar voice from behind him.

Rudi turned and squinted into the pink dawn beyond the crevice. "Mistress? Where are you going?"

"Up," said the Brixen Witch. She turned and began trudging away up the rocky path, dragging a small hatchet along the ground. In her hands it looked as huge as Marco's great axe.

"Wait!" Rudi scrambled to catch up with her. "You can't chop down the beanstalk!"

"True enough," she said. "I'm too old to be swinging an axe. You can do it. Come along, and step quick-like." She turned and started upslope once more.

"No!" cried Rudi. "What I mean to say is, we need the beanstalk."

"We?" said the witch, and now she noticed Agatha. "Who's this?" She inspected the girl as if she were some exotic butterfly. "From Petz, judging by the manner of dress. You're the one stole the Giant's beans?" It was not really a question.

Agatha squirmed under the little witch's gaze, and nodded.

The witch shifted her attention to Rudi. "I thought you were going to return them. And yet who did I hear stomping about outside my own front door just this morning? It *should* have been morning, at any rate. Grumbling about his stolen magic." She shook a finger at Rudi. "Did I not tell you that witches crossing borders would be disaster? Why did you not return his magic?"

"We did!" said Rudi. Now it was his turn to feel squirmy. "But then we stole this." He held up the burlap sack. Inside it, Not-Hildy clucked sleepily.

"You stole a chicken?"

"Yes, mistress."

"Whatever for?"

Rudi hesitated. "No good reason, mistress."

"You are telling me that the giant witch of Petz has finally dared to cross the border into Brixen, setting off all manner of mayhem, because of a chicken?"

"An enchanted chicken," explained Rudi. "Double-enchanted, really. She bears the Giant's keyhole mark. And then she ate a magic bean. And then—"

"And then this happened," said Agatha, stepping forward. She nudged Rudi, who produced the two golden eggs. They glimmered in the soft morning light.

"Solid gold," said the witch, weighing them in her hands. "Magic upon magic." The witch held out her hand. "What else do you have? Time is wasting."

Rudi and Agatha both stared blankly. "I didn't bring any—" began Rudi.

The witch bristled. "I'm not asking for tarts!" She turned her attention to Agatha. "Where are they? Do not defy a witch, girl. Empty your pocket."

Agatha dipped into her pocket and drew out a small pouch.

Rudi's mouth fell open at the sight. "The magic beans? You told me you returned them to the Giant's storehouse!"

"I meant to!" said Agatha. "But everything happened so quickly. The hens squawking in the yard, and Susanna shouting, and the Giant coming after us. I—I couldn't do it. I kept the beans, and we ran."

"So," declared the witch. "It seems we're piling up quite a collection of Petz magic. 'Tis more than even a second-rate witch can stand for. No wonder he has finally crossed the border."

Rudi stared at Agatha. "You lied to me!"

Agatha paled, but she stood her ground. "I had no choice! Stealing his magic is the only way to defeat him. I will not live my life in endless winter!"

A familiar pang of sympathy swirled around Rudi's anger and frustration. "There must be some other way," he said. "Isn't there, mistress? Can't you help?"

The witch cocked an eyebrow. "I told you once before, I has no power in Petz."

"So there it is," said Agatha. "No one can help me. Not even a witch. I'm sorry I lied to you, Rudi. But I'm not sorry I kept the beans."

Rudi rubbed his sweaty hands on his pants. "Please, mistress. The Giant is a tyrant. He's the one who's stolen, from the folk of Petz. He keeps them locked in winter, and near starving. He holds them prisoner in their own land. Agatha is only trying to gain back what is rightfully theirs. She escaped to Klausen on her own, even without a beanstalk."

The witch raised an eyebrow. "Is that so? How did you manage that, girl? The border of Petz is blocked by an enchantment."

"I had no trouble," Agatha protested. "The stories aren't true."

"*Hmph,*" said the witch, shaking the hatchet at Agatha. "There's no story that doesn't have a grain of truth, girl. That's what stories is for."

"Please, mistress," said Rudi. "Can't you give her any advice?"

"I just gave advice," said the witch. "Here's more: Rules is rules. No one can ignore the rules without paying the price. The folk of Petz has their witch, and must make do until such time as he is *not* their witch. Now, up that beanstalk with *all* the Giant's magic, before he comes down here again."

"But isn't *that* against the rules?" said Rudi. "The Giant coming to Brixen?"

"I should say so," declared the witch. "Now up you go, girl, because that infernal vine is coming down." She handed the golden eggs and the pouch of beans to Agatha, who pushed them deep into her pockets.

"I'm going too," said Rudi.

Agatha frowned at him. "You don't trust me, do you?"

Rudi's face burned, but he didn't care. "It doesn't matter, really. Petz is your concern, as it should be. But my concern is Brixen. And the only way for me to know that Brixen is safe from the foreign magic is to see for myself that it's returned properly. And so I'm going with you to Petz."

"'Tis decided, then," said the Brixen Witch. "But hurry back, Rudolf. That beanstalk is coming down at sunset." She paused and looked over her shoulder. "Or whenever I thinks sunset ought to be."

Now the witch turned to Agatha. "Take heart, child. Rules is rules, and nothing lasts forever. Pay attention, and your time will come. You has a choice." She waved them up the mountain once more. "Off with you now. And don't forget that there chicken!"

24

Rudi and Agatha hiked to the peak of the Berg in stony silence.

Before long, they arrived at the border. The beanstalk was still there, and so was the broken signpost, and the ice field that ended abruptly at the border. Everything looked exactly as Rudi and Susanna had left it.

Trying not to look at the spot where the snow finch had shattered and blown away, Rudi began to climb the beanstalk. He recalled his promise to Susanna— that he would tell Agatha about the snow finch—but just now he didn't feel like talking. So he climbed in silence, letting Not-Hildy's burlap sack swing gently from his belt.

Finally, from below him on the vine, Agatha said, "I am sorry, Rudi."

"No, you're not," Rudi shot back. "You said you're not."

"I wasn't before," she admitted. "But I am now. I didn't know the trouble it would cause." She was quiet for a moment. "I was thinking only of myself. And of Petz, of course. But now I know the world is bigger than that. And that everything is connected."

Rudi considered this, and decided it was a brave and honest thing to say. But it wasn't enough. "What else have you lied about?"

Agatha sputtered. "N-nothing!"

Rudi sighed in disappointment and exasperation. "What about the snow finch?"

"What snow finch?"

And so Rudi told Agatha about the snow finch, leaving out no detail. How the tiny, fragile bird had flitted across the enchanted border from Petz into Brixen, had turned to ice, and was gone.

Agatha gasped. "The poor thing!" There was a pause, and then in an awed whisper she said, "Just like in the stories."

"It's not a story," he said, a little too sharply. "It's true, and I've seen it. No one crosses the enchanted border unless the Giant permits it." Now he stopped and looked down at the top of Agatha's copper-colored head. "Not even you."

She swiped at the leaves that had fallen onto

her hair. "What are you saying, Rudi? Do you think the Giant *let* me cross the border with his magic beans?"

"I truly don't know," he answered. "But you had some kind of help. And you've already lied to me once. So why should I believe you about this?" He knew the words stung, but it couldn't be helped.

She looked up at him now, and her brown eyes did not waver from his gaze. "I will ask *you* why. If witches guard their magic so jealously, if one witch's magic in another witch's province causes so much trouble, then *why* would the Giant help me—or even *let* me—take his magic out of Petz?"

Rudi stared at her for a long moment, and his indignation sputtered. He couldn't think of a good reason why.

"I did lie about returning the beans," she said again. "And I've already told you, I'm truly sorry. But I haven't lied to you about anything else. I promise."

And he believed her, but he did not say so out loud. "Even so," he said. "How did you cross the border without turning to ice? Not even the smallest, most insignificant creature can do that."

Agatha only gave a pitiful shrug.

They climbed in silence once more, but this time it was a thoughtful silence. Gradually the vine tilted and became a level path. As they walked, Rudi filled his pockets with bean pods. He would give them to Ludwig as a gift. It was the least he could do.

"I liked your witch," ventured Agatha after a while. "Susanna was right about her. She can be testy, but she's kind. I wish Petz had a witch who was kind."

"Well," said Rudi absently as he picked at a tender pod and ate it. "The Brixen Witch did say that nothing lasts forever." As soon as he said this, the back of his neck tingled. He shuddered and brushed at his neck, wondering if a leaf had fallen from the vine. But there was nothing there.

"Ha!" said Agatha. "And where do you suppose we could find another witch? Because we could use one in Petz."

A memory nudged at Rudi. "The Brixen Witch explained once where a new witch comes from. She said it only takes someone with a gift for magic. It's not such a rare thing either." He felt his face burning. "Or so I'm told."

"Really?" said Agatha, who didn't seem to notice. "Do you know anyone with a gift for magic?"

Rudi gave a short laugh. "Oma says Susanna Louisa knows a magic bean when she sees one."

"Do *you* think Susanna Louisa might have the makings of a witch?"

Rudi's laugh became tangled with a cough. "I'm not sure."

Now Agatha laughed. "I thought your grandmother was a witch!"

"Just because she was with you when the beanstalk sprouted on the riverbank?'"

"Isn't that enough?" said Agatha. "She told me herself that no one else had been able to make it sprout. But there we were, just your Oma and I, and *whoosh*! Up it went. Very witchy, yes? Of course, that was before I met your real witch."

Now Rudi recalled how Susanna Louisa had thrown a bean onto the riverbank, expecting it to sprout, sure that it was magic. But it hadn't sprouted when she'd wanted it to.

So perhaps, despite her talents, Susanna Louisa did not quite have the makings of a witch after all.

How did a person become a witch, then, if it wasn't enough to be born with a gift for magic? Practice? Patience? Paying attention? Perhaps all of those things.

"Mayhaps your Oma *is* a witch," said Agatha, waking Rudi from his thoughts. "Or would be, if you didn't already have a witch." She plucked a tender bean pod and smiled at Rudi. The first genuine smile he'd seen from her. It made his heart leap.

The beanstalk became a ladder once more. Soon they would be in Petz. Inside her burlap sack Not-Hildy gave a contented cluck, as if she knew she was almost home.

And then, all at once, their feet touched solid ground. It was exactly where Rudi remembered it would be—below the village, behind a stand of wind-battered pines. Rudi and Agatha bundled themselves against the bitter cold and trooped up the icy slope, past the weather-beaten houses adorned with mistletoe.

Rudi thought again of how Agatha had lied about the magic beans. Now, as they walked through the bleak and frozen landscape, he forgave her utterly. How could he blame Agatha for wanting the summer back? Especially when it had been stolen by a selfish and hateful witch?

They arrived at Ludwig's cottage, and the reunion was everything Rudi had imagined it would be: tears and hugs and shouts of joy. Ludwig thanked Rudi for the bean pods, and for seeing his daughter safely home. Rudi thanked Ludwig, too, and returned the mittens and the scarf and the fur-lined hat. Ludwig insisted that Rudi keep the hat, as a token of thanks from the good folk of Petz. Rudi accepted the gift but would not accept a meal, or even a cup of tea. He had an errand to finish, and he needed to return home before sundown.

"I'll let you two say your good-byes, then," said Ludwig. He shook Rudi's hand, smothered him in a fleeting hug, and was gone inside the house.

"I will take the Giant's things," Rudi told Agatha. "There's no need for you to worry your father any more."

She frowned. "It doesn't seem right to send you to finish what I started."

"I don't mind," said Rudi. "It's the least I can do,

since I wasn't able to help you get your summer back."

Agatha gave him the magic beans, and the eggs, and Not-Hildy, who dozed peacefully in her warm sack as if she were under an enchantment. "Don't blame yourself," she said. "I suppose it was not meant to be. But Brixen is safe. I'm home again with Papa. I'm content with that." And Rudi was sure she meant it, though her smile had lost its brightness.

"Well, then," he said, shuffling his feet. He suddenly remembered how he'd daydreamed about kissing her good-bye. Now that the moment had come, he realized what a silly idea it was. "I'm glad to have met you. And I don't care what it looks like around here. Petz is a nice place." He offered his hand, and Agatha shook it briefly. Her hand was warm, despite the cold.

"I'm off, then," he said.

"You remember the way?"

"Yes. I just need the key." Rudi held out his hand once more.

Agatha blinked at him. "I don't have the key. You have the key."

They stared at each other for a moment, their breath rising in clouds around their heads.

Then Rudi remembered. "We left it! We left it in the doorway."

"Now what?" said Agatha. "Will it still be there? Or has he found it? How will you get in?"

Rudi swallowed his panic. They had been through too much to be defeated now. *Think,* he told himself. *Pay attention. You weren't born with the talent. But you've learned. You are equal to the task.*

And then he remembered something else, and suddenly everything made sense.

"Agatha," said Rudi. "The Brixen Witch said that some people are born with a gift for magic. And some of *those* people learn better than others how to use that gift."

She brushed a strand of copper-colored hair out of her face. "What are you talking about, Rudi?"

"The Brixen Witch also told us that nothing lasts forever. And that rules is rules."

"What rules?"

"Rules for magic. One witch at a time."

"Yes?" She rubbed her hands to warm them.

Rudi glanced around him quickly. There was no one else in the snowy lane. "Agatha, how did you cross the border without meeting the snow finch's fate?"

She shook her head, confused. "I already told you, I don't know."

"And how did the beanstalk sprout on the riverbank? When you and Oma were there together?"

"I don't know that, either. It just . . . happened."

"No," he said, stomping his feet in the cold. "Something caused it to sprout. Think. What happened? Remember every detail."

Agatha frowned in concentration. "We were walking past the footbridge," she said. "Your Oma was showing me which way you'd gone. She told me to find you and then to hurry on home so my family wouldn't worry . . . and that made me think about Papa. . . ." She looked up at Rudi, her eyes wide. "And then the beanstalk sprouted. *Whoosh!*"

Rudi stared back at her. "Only a witch could have done that," he said. "And if there's one thing I've learned, it's this: My grandmother is *not* a witch."

25

Agatha squinted at him. Her face had gone pale. "Rudi," she whispered, "are you saying that *I*—"

"You have a gift, Agatha," he said in a rush. "The beanstalk on the riverbank. Escaping from Petz on your own. You performed an enchantment, and you disarmed an enchantment already put forth. And what about the cats? And Zick-Zack!"

"But . . . it can't be that simple, can it?"

"Why not?" he said. "Perhaps you're not an actual witch. But I think you *could* be one." Then he stopped to catch his breath. "That is, if you're willing."

You has a choice, the Brixen Witch had said.

Now Rudi looked into Agatha's brown eyes. "It's a big responsibility, though. I think that once you decide, there may be no changing your mind.

And you'd never be able to leave Petz, I suppose."

Suddenly Rudi realized what he was suggesting. To be witch of your province meant more than simply paying attention. It required endless vigilance. It meant presiding over a thousand scattered lives. Listening to the mountain breathe. Knowing the steps of every lamb in your province, and the flutter of every wing. To say that it was a big responsibility was like saying a blizzard contained a few snowflakes. He was suggesting to Agatha a lifetime of care and worry. Several lifetimes, perhaps.

"You'd be a very capable witch, though," he heard himself saying. And he knew it was true.

"Me?" she said again, and then her face clouded and she stole a glance through the cottage window. "What about Papa?"

Rudi thought for a moment. "He could be your adviser." Even as he said it, Rudi knew that Ludwig would be equal to that task.

"Is that allowed?" asked Agatha.

"Why not? There are rules, it's true. But I've never heard of a rule about where a witch must live, or who her advisers should be."

Agatha frowned and bit her lip. She rubbed her arms vigorously against the cold. "You're telling me that Petz can be freed of its tyrant? Once and for all?"

Rudi nodded.

She looked all around her—at the crooked houses with their faded shutters; at the feeble spirals of smoke rising from the crumbling chimneys; at the hard-packed, snowy ground that was as gray as the sky.

And then she smiled, another genuine smile. She opened the door of the cottage and leaned inside. "Papa!" she called. "I'm going for a walk!"

They made their plans as they hiked up through the village.

"What if the key is gone?" said Agatha. "How will we get in?"

"We'll use a bean. *You'll* use a bean," he said. "And I have a feeling that will be enough."

And so it was. Though the small door into the fortress was locked again, and bolted for good measure, it opened under Agatha's hand as if it had been waiting for her. They stepped inside the Giant's fortress, and the warm scents of wild roses and new grass washed over them.

Once again they crept between the wall and the hedge until they came to the Giant's back meadow. As quickly and gently as they could, they released Not-Hildy to the familiar confines of her yard. She immediately began to scratch and cluck, as if all her adventures had been a burlap-colored dream.

The storehouse was locked too, but Agatha made quick work of opening the door. They shook the magic beans from their pouch onto the huge mound of key-hole beans piled in one corner. They set the golden eggs there too.

"Ready?" said Rudi to Agatha.

"No!" she whispered, grasping his arm. "I thought I was, but am I? What do I need to do? How will we know if . . . if it works?"

Rudi did his best to sound reassuring. "I have a feeling that if it happens, we'll know it. Wait here, where he can't see you, until I've had time to get back to the beanstalk. Don't worry," he added. "I know you are equal to the task."

With that, Rudi walked out of the storehouse and along the low stone wall that enclosed the Giant's back garden. He stood at the gate and stared at the grand house, gathering his courage. He rubbed the back of his hand. The scraped knuckle had already begun to heal, and at any rate it hadn't been much of a scrape. No worse than the daily scratches and bruises he collected while working on Papa's farm. Milk buckets, fence posts, bad-tempered cats. What was another scrape, more or less?

In one swift motion Rudi swept his knuckles across the rough stone of the wall. He felt a mild sting as the scab tore away and the small wound opened. It oozed the tiniest drop of blood.

He didn't have to wait long.

FUM. . . .

Rudi smiled with satisfaction, and ran for his life.

He had crossed the meadow and reached the hedge before he realized that he hadn't wished Agatha a proper good-bye.

He had wrenched open the small door in the wall of the fortress and propped it open with a rock before he also remembered that he might never see her again.

FUM. . . .

He had charged down the slope, through the village of Petz, past Ludwig's crooked cottage and an assortment of startled villagers, before he decided that, though Agatha would be bound by the rules of magic and never be allowed to venture outside Petz herself, there was really no reason why he couldn't come back to visit her one day. He would have to go the long way, of course. But it could be done. And when the new witch had restored the summer to Petz, and the seasons were once again in their proper order, it would most likely be quite a pleasant place to visit.

FUM. . . . FUMM. . . .

Rudi found the beanstalk behind the clump of wind-blown trees and began to climb. Would the Giant follow him this time?

In a moment the beanstalk began to shake and sway, and Rudi knew. As he scrambled along the inside of the beanstalk, he could see the Giant's shadow through the green vines, following him on the outside. They raced along the beanstalk, up, and then horizontally, and finally down. The Giant's shadow was always just behind Rudi.

By the time they reached the other end of the beanstalk, at the border of Brixen and Petz, the Giant's shadow had blended with a twilight that Rudi knew had come too early.

In the dusk at the peak of the Berg, someone was waiting for them.

"Who goes there?" said the Brixen Witch as Rudi hurried to stand by her side. "Who is trespassing in my backyard?" She raised a hand. There was a sudden flare of light, which settled into a steady golden glow of lamplight. At her feet lay her little hatchet.

"You know who I am!" bellowed the Giant. He dropped from the beanstalk into the circle of lamplight, crushing what remained of the signpost that had once pointed toward Brixen in one direction and Petz in the other.

And now, for the first time, Rudi had a clear view of the witch of Petz. Rudi didn't know what he'd expected. But he had not expected this.

He looked for all the world like an ordinary man. He was perhaps as old as Papa, and he was dressed in rough woolens. The only extraordinary thing about him was his size. Standing there, on the edge of the ice field that marked the border of Petz, he looked as tall as three men, at least.

"You are harboring a thief!" roared the Giant.

"A thief?" said the witch innocently. "Whatever did he steal from you that makes you come all this way after him?"

"Ask him yourself," answered the Giant, pointing at Rudi. "This time you're caught, thief! Give it back!"

"This?" said Rudi, holding up a small oval object. It glimmered in the lamplight. "It's only one golden egg. A mere fraction of all the wealth and magic you possess."

"What has you done now?" hissed the Brixen Witch. "Bringing Petz magic to Brixen again?"

"Don't worry," whispered Rudi, and he showed her. It was the brown egg Susanna had given him, shimmering like gold in the lamplight. "The Giant is so angry, and so busy chasing *me*, that he hasn't noticed that all his magic is back in Petz."

The little witch squinted at him, and the beginnings of a smile appeared on her wrinkled face. "Clever lad."

The Giant stepped off the ice and onto the bare rocky ground of Brixen. He did not, Rudi noticed with a vague disappointment, turn to ice. A few more steps, and the witch of Petz would be upon them.

Now Rudi's mouth fell open, and he stared in astonishment. For as the Giant drew nearer, he seemed to shrink in size. When he finally stood in front of them, he was only a few inches taller than Rudi.

At the same time, the blackness at the edge of the lamplight faded away into daylight.

It's happening, thought Rudi. *The witch of Petz has abandoned his post. His power is waning.*

Rudi imagined the summer flowing out of the Giant's fortress through the small open doorway, and over the high stone wall, covering all of Petz like a soft green blanket. He imagined the new witch emerging from the storehouse and throwing open the dark shutters of the grand manor, letting in the sunshine and fresh air. And he wished he could be there to see it for himself. But for now it was enough to imagine it, and to believe it must be true.

The Brixen Witch nudged Rudi. "Give me the egg and take the hatchet," she whispered, never taking her gaze from the once-giant man.

Rudi did what she had asked. Then, as the Brixen Witch kept up her conversation with the diminished Giant, Rudi crept past them with the hatchet in his hand.

"'Tis not real gold, I'm afraid," the witch was saying. "But 'tis tasty, I'll wager. Would you like me to fry it up for you?"

The Giant raised a fist. "You know who I am," he snarled again. "I am a witch as powerful as you!"

"Is that so?" said the witch. "You seems to be losing your steam."

Now the Giant stopped. He looked himself up and down. He stared at the Brixen Witch in horror. They were nearly eye to eye. "What have you done?" he cried.

"'Tis not myself," she said. "'Tis simply the rules. Once, you were a witch. But you has left your province unattended, and it seems someone else was ready to take your place. You are relieved of your duty."

The man from Petz—for that was all he was now—opened his mouth in fury, but then his brow smoothed. "I'm so tired." He blinked at the Brixen Witch as if seeing her for the first time. "I do like a nice fried egg."

"Come along, then," she said. "I see the spring nettles is sprouted. They'll make a lovely cup of tea. Nice and tender. Hardly any sting to 'em at all this time of year." And the Brixen Witch led the weary traveler down the slope.

Rudi scratched his ear. "I think she's really going to fry him an egg," he said to himself.

He turned his attention to the task at hand. It was a small hatchet, and it would take some time to finish the job.

As Rudi prepared to take the first swing, something came fluttering down the beanstalk, deep pink against the green of the leaves.

A flower. A wild hedge rose.

"Clever girl," said Rudi, tucking it into his pocket.

26

In Brixen, the spring blossomed into summer.

The last patches of snow melted. The days grew longer, and the hours were marked by roosters crowing, by cows demanding to be milked, and by the bells of the steeple clock.

The villagers of Brixen ate their fill of beans, and planted more, for a bumper crop that would continue to provide for many seasons to come.

Rosie's calf, Daisy, grew strong and healthy, and now the Bauer dairy had four cows, which was better than three.

Marco the blacksmith took on a new apprentice. He was a quiet fellow, emigrated all the way from Petz. He had no family there, he said, and couldn't even recall why he had stayed so long. He had finally moved on, and had never been more content. He owned an iron key just like the ones Marco forged. He was quite fond of fried eggs.

No one ever spoke again of the golden eggs. It was bad luck to talk of such things.

But Brixen folk love a good story, and so stories were told that summer, during the long, mild evenings, of once-frozen lands across the mountains, and cracking ice, and thawing ground such as hadn't been seen in many a long year.

Konrad claimed to hear stories of a foreign witch. A giant, a witch-king, a *hexenmeister*, who became too greedy and who finally met a bad end when a worthy challenger fought him to a bloody and gruesome death. Konrad told the story to Roger, who told it to Nicolas, who said it was ridiculous, and so he told Rudi, who told no one at all.

Susanna Louisa had been waiting for Rudi, just as she had promised. And every day she brought him a fresh brown egg laid by Hildy, her very own hen. Sometimes, if the light was right, the egg looked as if it were made of gold.

As for Rudi, he milked the cows and planted beans. He picked ripe elderberries for Mama to bake into tarts. From time to time he visited the old woman who lived on the mountain. They shared stories, and tea, and elderberry tarts. On market days Rudi walked to

Klausen, where he saw no furtive red-haired girls, and he told himself he was glad.

He became accustomed to the sidelong glances from his neighbors and the whispers behind his back. He told himself it was a mark of respect. Some things you are born with, he decided. And other things you learn. But it's what you're good at that matters. Rudi was good with cows. He was good with witches.

"Do you suppose the new apprentice blacksmith remembers much about his life in Petz?" Rudi asked Oma one day as they stirred their tea.

"George?" She tapped her foot and rocked in her chair. "I don't know. I daresay he's better off not remembering. Marco tells me he's settling in nicely, though."

"I wonder how things are in Petz." Rudi had so many other questions. Was Agatha happy? Were she and Ludwig adjusting to their new life?

"Look around you," said Oma, patting his cheek. "See how ordinary and quiet everything is?"

Rudi nodded. "I like it that way."

"So you should. It means all is right with the world. As long as we don't see anything as strange as keyhole beans, or giant beanstalks, or golden-egg-laying chickens, I should think that things in Petz are just fine too."

Rudi thought about this for a moment. His gaze wandered out the window and toward the looming peak of the Berg. "You're probably right," he said.

Oma sipped her tea thoughtfully. "Sometimes," she said, squinting at him through the steam, "the best way to know something is to find out for yourself."

"Quite true," said Rudi. He took a bite of elder-berry tart.

"It's high summer," said Oma. "The days are long. The weather is mild. A good time for traveling, I should think."

Rudi slipped a hand into his pocket and patted the dried rose blossom that nestled within. "I was thinking the same thing myself. Perhaps you could bake a few extra elderberry tarts?"